OKLAHOMA
OUTBREAK

Here's what readers from around the country are saying about Johnathan Rand's AMERICAN CHILLERS:

"When you came to my school in October of 2007, everyone knew you'd be good, but no one knew you'd be amazing! Until the end of the school year EVERYONE read your books, and next year I bet everyone will continue to read them! Thanks for an AMAZING presentation!"

-David N., age 11, Pennsylvania

"I used to not like to read, but after reading one of your books, I could not stop reading them. I am going to read all of your books!"

-Hunter O., age 12, Michigan

"I love your books! I just finished with HAUNTING IN NEW HAMPSHIRE! I got really scared. I can't wait for your next book!"

-Trevor H., age 8, Washington

"I got so freaked out when I read TERRIFYING TOYS OF TENNESSEE, and I don't even live in Tennessee. Your books are the best!"

-Amber P., age 12, North Carolina

"A couple of weeks ago, I read TERRIBLE TRACTORS OF TEXAS. It was cool when the tractors came to life! It was great!

-Sonny B., age 9, Michigan

"My mom and dad bought me one of your books, but I wanted a kitten. But the book was great, and I loved it!

-Kris T., age 11, Texas

"Dude, your books are the coolest. I used to think reading was boring, but your books aren't! Write faster!"
                                                    -Greg G., age 9, Alaska

"I got seven of your books for my birthday. That was last month, and I've read all of them. I can't wait to get more!"
                                                    -Jon L., age 12, Nevada

"My sister used to read your books to me, and I thought they were cool. Now, I read them on my own, and I LOVE them!"
                                                    -Javon E., age 10, Illinois

"My first book I read was MISSOURI MADHOUSE. It was funny, cool, and scary. Not too scary, but just right."
                                                    -Alissa M., age 11, Michigan

"My dad and I read WICKED VELOCIRAPTORS OF WEST VIRGINIA. We both loved it, which is great, because my dad just bought me four more of your books!"
                                                    -Derek S., age 8, Florida

"MISSISSIPPI MEGALODON is the best book in the world. How did you come up with that book? It scared the heck out of me. I don't think I'll ever go swimming again."
                                                    -Dani M., age 10, Mississippi

"My friends and I love your books so much that we formed an American Chillers book club. We meet every week and make bookmarks and posters. You can come anytime, if you want. Your books are the coolest in the world!"
                                                    -Carter F., age 11, Indiana

"I don't know what it is about your books, but they're the only ones I read. They're so good, I've read some of them twice!"

-Gabe L., age 9, New York

"All my friends were reading your books, and I didn't know what the big deal was, until I read one. Now, I love them, too!"

-Jessica O., age 8, Nebraska

"If you make movies about your books, can I be in them? I don't even want any money or nothing."

-Alex F., age 9, Kentucky

"My grandma bought me some of your books at your store, Chillermania. I had never read any of them before, but now I can't stop reading them!"

-Andrew R., age 11, Maine

"I have read every single American Chillers book except MISSISSIPPI MEGALODON. You write great books!"

-Zachary R., age 9, Michigan

"I love to read your books at night, under the covers, with a flashlight. I get really creeped out!"

-Britney., age 10, Louisiana

Got something cool to say about Johnathan Rand's books? Let us know, and we might publish it right here! Send your short blurb to:
Chiller Blurbs
281 Cool Blurbs Ave.
Topinabee, MI 49791

Don't miss these exciting, action-packed books by Johnathan Rand:

AMERICAN CHILLERS

America's #1 Series for MAXIMUM Chills!

#26:
Oklahoma
Outbreak

Johnathan Rand

An AudioCraft Publishing, Inc. book

This book is a work of fiction. Names, places, characters and incidents are used fictitiously, or are products of the author's very active imagination.

Book storage and warehouses provided by Chillermania!©
Indian River, Michigan

Warehouse security provided by:
Lily Munster, Scooby-Boo & Spooky Dude

American Chillers #26: Oklahoma Outbreak
ISBN 13-digit: 978-1-893699-99-1

Librarians/Media Specialists:
PCIP/MARC records available **free of charge** at
www.americanchillers.com

Cover illustration by Dwayne Harris
Cover layout and design by Sue Harring

Dickinson Press Inc. Grand Rapids, MI USA Job # 38939 06/20/2011

OKLAHOMA
OUTBREAK

VISIT CHILLERMANIA!

WORLD HEADQUARTERS FOR BOOKS BY JOHNATHAN RAND!

Yooperland

Indian River

Alpena

Traverse City

MICHIGAN

CHILLERMANIA!

*I-75 Exit 313
then south
1 mile!*

Mt. Pleasant

Bay City

Grand Rapids

Lansing

Detroit

Kalamazoo

Visit the HOME for books by Johnathan Rand! Featuring books, hats, shirts, bookmarks and other cool stuff not available anywhere else in the world! Plus, watch the American Chillers website for news of special events and signings at *CHILLERMANIA!* with author Johnathan Rand! Located in northern lower Michigan, on I-75! Take exit 313 . . . then south 1 mile! For more info, call (231) 238-0338. And be afraid! Be veeeery afraaaaaaiiiid . . . .

Monday at school was just like any other day in Tulsa, Oklahoma. The bell rang at exactly eight-thirty. I had exactly two minutes to get to my classroom.

But in those two minutes, something happened that would set the stage for an unbelievable series of events . . . turning an otherwise normal day into what could only be described as a horrifying roller coaster ride of terror.

"Tricia! Hey, Tricia! Wait up!"

When I heard my name being called, I turned. Of course, I'd already recognized the voice. It was Carlos Marcos, a friend I've known since first grade.

The hall was packed with dozens of other chattering, laughing students, scurrying like ants to their classrooms. Carlos was weaving through the hoard, snaking around kids as he made his way toward me. I took a few steps to the side so I wouldn't be standing in the middle of the hallway and leaned against a locker.

Carlos came up to me. He had his backpack slung over his shoulder, and his shoes were untied, like usual. Like usual, I had to remind him to tie them. One of these days he was going to trip, fall, and land square on his face.

"Hey," Carlos said.

"Hey, yourself," I replied, and I pointed to his shoes.

"Oh, yeah," he said, and he knelt down to tie them. While he worked with the laces, he looked up at me and spoke. "Did you read chapter seven?" he asked. His eyes were wide with excitement.

I nodded. "I'm way past that," I said. "In fact, I'm all the way up to chapter fifteen. The book is really freaky."

"I can't wait for book club tonight," Carlos said, getting to his feet.

"Me, too," I replied. "I can't wait to finish the book. Last night, I read beneath the covers with a flashlight, and my mom and dad never knew it."

Carlos and I are in a book club with ten other students. All of us love to read, and with the help of Mrs. Candor, the school media specialist, we formed an after school book club. Every month, we choose a book for all of us to read, on our own, and we get together every Monday after school to discuss it. It's a blast. Not only do we read some really cool books, but it's fun to get together with friends to talk about the story we're reading. Mrs. Candor usually brings snacks like cookies or cupcakes, which is cool.

Just then, Tommy Gersky, carrying his blue folder with homework, emerged from the throng of hustling students. He's in our book club, too.

"Hey, guys," he said.

"Hi, Tommy," I replied.

"How's it going?" Carlos asked.

"Cool as butter," Tommy replied with a wink. That's a phrase he always says, and he always winks

13

when he says it. When things were going well, he always said everything was as 'cool as butter.' Which is a little strange, being that butter isn't always cool.

Regardless, things might have been as 'cool as butter' at that moment, but in less than five seconds, 'cool as butter' was going to turn into icy terror . . . and it all started when a girl accidentally bumped into Tommy.

2

Tommy was just about to say something, when he was suddenly knocked forward. He dropped his folder, and papers spilled out all over the floor. He snapped around angrily to see Brianna Carson. She's also part of our book club.

She had a shocked look on her face. "I'm so sorry," she said. "I wasn't looking."

"Watch where you're going," Tommy snapped. He rubbed his arms and shoulders like he was brushing something off. "That's how cooties are spread," he said. "I've probably got cooties all over me, now."

"I don't have cooties!" Brianna said. She

sounded hurt.

"That's because you gave them all to me," Tommy taunted, still brushing the imaginary cooties from his arms and shoulders.

"I said I was sorry," Brianna said. She stormed off, vanishing into a sea of other students.

"That wasn't very nice," I said to Tommy.

"Yeah," Carlos agreed.

"Hey, she ran into me," Tommy replied as he knelt down to gather up his papers and folder. "Besides . . . I was only kidding."

"Still, it wasn't very nice," I said.

Tommy was indifferent. "She'll get over it," he replied. "It's not like I punched her, or anything."

Now, Tommy isn't a bad kid, but sometimes, he says things without thinking. I think everyone does, once in a while. But he doesn't realize little comments like that can hurt people's feelings.

Regardless, the matter was dropped. Tommy headed to his classroom, Carlos went to his, and I went to mine. We're all in sixth grade, but we all have different classrooms. It would have been fun if all three of us had the same teacher, but we didn't. I had Mr. Billings. He was really nice, but he always gave us way too much homework . . . especially on the weekends.

The day passed like any other. I had lunch with Tommy and Carlos in the cafeteria, and I went to gym class and the library. When the bell rang and classes got out, I was relieved that Mr. Billings hadn't given us any homework at all. It would have been hard, being that I had book club to go to, which usually lasts a couple of hours.

It was three o'clock. Book club started in thirty minutes. Usually, I meet Tommy and Carlos in the hall next to my locker, which is where I found Tommy waiting for me.

"I forgot my book at home," he said, "and they don't have any extra copies in the library."

I shrugged. "It doesn't matter. We won't be doing any reading. We'll just be talking about the book. And Mrs. Candor told me earlier that she brought us chocolate chip cookies!"

"Cool as butter," Tommy said.

Carlos arrived a couple minutes later. His shoes were untied again, and he looked puzzled. Worried, even.

"Something's wrong," he said as he walked up to us.

"Of course something's wrong," Tommy said. "Your shoes are untied again."

Carlos looked at his feet and knelt down to tie them.

"No," he said, looking up as his fingers worked the laces. "I mean, with Brianna. I just saw her on my way here. She was in the library, and she looked sick."

"What do you mean?" I asked. "Like, she caught a cold or something?"

Carlos finished tying his shoes and stood. He shook his head. "It's worse than that," he said. "I only saw her for a moment. She looked really pale, and there were dark circles around her eyes. And another kid in our book club—Wayne—he looked sick, too. I think they might have the flu. I hope it's not going around."

Carlos was right about one thing: Brianna and Wayne were sick, all right.

But it wasn't the flu.

It wasn't a cold or anything like it. In fact, the illness was caused by something that, up until then, I thought had been made-up.

A joke.

But it wasn't.

The illness was real, and so was the cause of it. *Cooties.*

We didn't know it at the time, but the dangerous cootie infection had already spread to other students in our school, and there was no stopping it.

The Oklahoma Outbreak had begun.

3

We chatted in the hall for a moment, listening to the sounds of the school emptying: slamming lockers, laughter, talking, shoes scuffing the tile floor, friends calling out to friends. There was an announcement on the school public address system, saying that the Monday afternoon book club would begin in twenty five minutes in the library.

"If Brianna and Wayne are sick," I said, "they'll miss book club."

"That means more chocolate chip cookies for us," Tommy replied, rubbing his belly. "I love chocolate chip cookies."

"But what if they're *really* sick?" I wondered aloud. "What if they have to go to the hospital? That would be awful."

"I don't know where they went," Carlos said, "but I'm sure they won't be at book club. I'll bet they went home. They looked like they crawled out of their own coffins."

"Come on," I said. "Let's head for the library. It's early, but the rest of the group is probably waiting. If the rest of the group is there, maybe we can start early."

"And start packing in the cookies," Tommy said, rubbing his belly again. He sniffed the air. "I can almost smell them from here."

We walked down the hall. Carlos carried his backpack, and I carried my books. Tommy's folder was tucked beneath his arm.

"It's weird to be here after school has let out," I said. "It's so quiet."

The halls were empty, and the lights had been turned out. A few teachers had gone home for the day, but a few remained in their classrooms. A few pieces of paper were on the floor, but the custodian, Mr. Jones, would have the place cleaned up soon.

And the only sound we heard was the scuffing of our shoes on the tile floor.

"It's almost spooky," Carlos said. "The school is completely different when no one else is around."

"Hey, that would make a good book," Tommy said. "Someone could write a story about a haunted school."

"Why don't you write it?" I asked.

"Maybe I will," Tommy replied. "I'll write a book about the three of us being in our school with ghosts. I'll make it super-scary, just like the book we're reading right now for book club. I'll make it the scariest book anyone's ever read."

Which, of course, was unlikely. There wasn't a single book written that could be as scary as what was about to happen to us in the library.

There were a couple of things that should have alerted us to the fact that something was wrong.

First, the lights were off in the library. Usually, they're left on for book club. Our library is really cool, too. There are paintings on the walls, featuring characters from popular books. A bunch of stuffed animals sit on the bookshelves. It's not cold and stale, like some libraries. It's colorful and lively.

Today, however, the library was dark. We could make out the silhouettes and shadows of tables and bookshelves, but the entire library was gloomy and cheerless.

Second, there wasn't anyone else around. Usually, there are at least one or two members of our book club waiting for the rest of us to arrive. Today, no one was in sight. Not even Mrs. Candor.

"This is strange," I said, trying the library door. I thought it might be locked, but it wasn't. I pulled it open and stepped inside. Carlos and Tommy followed.

"Hello?" I called out. "Anyone here?"

"Even Mrs. Candor's office is dark," Carlos said.

"Great," Tommy said, rubbing his hands together. "Let's find those chocolate chip cookies and dig in."

"We're not eating any cookies until everyone gets here," I said. "Besides . . . I don't even smell any cookies. Maybe Mrs. Candor isn't even here, yet."

I reached out and turned the lights on. Shadows scattered and vanished, and the characters and creatures painted on the walls came to life in a sea of bright, happy colors and wide smiles. On the far wall, an enormous red dog sat, grinning at a small girl no bigger than his paw. On the wall to my right, a happy monkey rode a bicycle, while wild things paraded about, dancing and prancing and creating a rumpus. On the left wall, there was a painting of a plump yellow bear with his head in a honey jar. Next to him was a family of mice in a leaf, floating in a river. There was also a painting of a small boy standing atop an enormous peach. I don't know who created the art work, but it sure made the library look cool.

"It's odd that no one is here, yet," Carlos said, looking around.

"Maybe they changed the meeting place and didn't tell us," Tommy said.

I shook my head and pulled a lock of hair away from my face. "No," I replied. "The announcement just a few minutes ago said that book club was meeting here in the library in twenty five minutes."

I looked at the clock on the wall. It was almost ten minutes after three. Mrs. Candor should still be in her office.

This is really strange, I thought. *This place is completely empty.*

We heard a noise and turned around. The library door was opening . . . but it wasn't Mrs. Candor. It wasn't one of the kids in our book club.

It was a zombie!

5

What came through the door couldn't possibly be human. It couldn't possibly be alive . . . but it *was*.

But I had been wrong about one thing: it *was* a human. In fact, it was *Wayne*. And he looked horrifying, not like himself at all, which is why it took me a moment to recognize him.

His arms, hands, neck, and face were completely white. There were dark circles around his eyes, and they looked sunken and empty. There was a red mark on his cheek that was swollen and bruised. He had red marks on his hands and arms, too. Wayne has short, brown hair that he usually keeps neatly combed. Now, it was messy, sticking out in all different directions, like he just got out of bed.

And *bugs*.

There were black bugs, about the size of a quarter, crawling on him! He had two in his hair, one on his shoulder, and one on his bare arm. It was obvious Wayne was more than just sick. Something was really, really wrong with him.

When he saw us, he stopped and stared. His eyes were wild, like an angry, caged animal.

"W . . . Wayne?" Carlos stammered. "Is . . . is that . . . *you?*"

Wayne responded with a throaty moan and a low growl. His mouth opened, and I gasped when I saw his teeth. They were all yellow and rotting away.

This isn't real, I told myself. *It's not possible.*

"Man, you look awful," Tommy said. "Have you checked yourself out in a mirror? You got a bad case of the uglies."

Wayne's lip curled, and he let out a low snarl. Then, he slowly raised both his arms, reaching for us.

"Hey, I didn't mean to make you mad," Tommy said, raising his hands and showing his palms. "But you really *do* look bad."

I took a step back, and so did Carlos and Tommy.

Wayne took a step forward. Drool came out of the left side of his mouth and dribbled down his chin.

Then, he began speaking.

"Kooooo," he said. *"Kooooo . . . kooooo . . . ."*

"Wayne?" I said as I took yet another step back. "Wayne . . . what's wrong? What's happened to you?"

"Kooooo . . . kooooo . . . teeeeez . . . ."

"What are you saying?" Carlos asked. His voice trembled, and he took a step backward. Tommy stepped backward, bumped into a table, then backed around it. None of us wanted Wayne to get any closer.

"He looks like he's got the flu or something," I said.

"What are those things crawling all over him?" Tommy asked. "They look like black grasshoppers."

"Kooooo . . . teeeeez," Wayne replied in a low, animal-like growl. *"Kooooo . . . teeeeez . . . ."*

"I don't understand what he's saying," Carlos said.

Of course, if we had thought about it, we would have figured out what he was saying. However, at the time, my mind was too busy trying to figure out what was going on.

What's wrong with him? I wondered. *He's sick, obviously. But what if he gets near us? Will we catch what he has?*

"He needs help," I said.

At that very moment, Wayne lunged for us, and I realized something: Wayne wasn't the one that needed help . . . we were.

6

Wayne attacked.

He wasn't moving very quickly, but, rather, shuffling and stumbling along like I'd seen Frankenstein do in those old movies. His arms were outstretched in front of him, and his hands were grasping at air.

It didn't take but a split second for the three of us to figure out what to do.

"Let's get out of here!" Tommy shouted. *"I don't want him anywhere near me!"*

The three of us sprang at once. I wasn't paying attention, and I ran right into a table and fell to the ground. I quickly leapt to my feet, following Tommy and Carlos as they darted around tables and bookshelves, headed for the set of doors at the other end of the library that opened into another hallway.

"Man, this is whacked out!" Tommy shrieked. *"Wayne has lost his mind! He's like a zombie or something!"*

We ran until we made it to the other side of the library. Carlos was going so fast that he couldn't stop, and he slammed into a bookshelf, knocking several books and a stuffed animal to the floor. Tommy grabbed the door handle, gave it a frantic turn, and pushed. The door opened, and we bolted into the hallway.

But Wayne was quicker than I'd thought. He was only a few steps behind us and was reaching for the doors.

I looked up and down the hall. By now, all of the teachers had left. Classroom lights were off, and several doors were closed. However, directly across the hall, a classroom door was open.

"In there!" Carlos shouted. "Let's get in the classroom and lock the door!"

In three gigantic bounds, we were in the room.

Tommy pushed the door shut.

"Lock it!" Carlos shouted.

Tommy shook his head in bewilderment as he fumbled with the knob. "I can't!" he said. "It won't lock! You have to have a key!"

Suddenly, Wayne slammed into the other side of the door. Through the window, we could see his white face; his dark, sinister eyes; and the red wound on his cheek. And the bugs on his skin! He looked so gross. Our friend had turned into a monster from beyond the grave.

Still, I felt sorry for him. He needed help, but we had to worry about saving ourselves first. We certainly didn't want to catch what he had!

On the other side of the door, Wayne grabbed the knob and tried to push it open, in an effort to force his way in. Tommy was pressed against the door, using his weight to keep it shut.

"Help me!" he shouted.

Carlos and I sprang, pressing our bodies against the door to keep Wayne out. All the while, Wayne pushed and slapped at the door, trying to get in.

But he was no match for the three of us, thankfully. Together, we were much stronger than he was. After a minute of struggling and trying to push the door open, he backed away. We watched him turn and stumble away. Soon, he had vanished down the hall, and the three of us backed away from the door.

"I'm glad that's over," Tommy said with a sigh of relief.

But, as you might have guessed, it wasn't over. Not even close.

Without warning, another body slammed into the door. I caught a glimpse of blonde hair and a flash of red clothing.

The three of us leapt to try to keep the door closed, but it was too late. The door burst open, and there was nothing we could do as the body tumbled through the doorway and ran into the three of us, knocking us all backward and causing us to fall to the floor.

I knocked over a desk before I hit the floor, wincing in pain as my elbow struck the hard tile. I heard another desk crash as it fell over. Someone yelped, but I couldn't tell if it was Carlos or Tommy.

Quickly, I got to my feet, ready to defend myself. Carlos and Tommy, too, were quick to leap up.

Our attacker stood up. She didn't have pasty-white skin or dark circles around her eyes. She didn't have any bugs in her hair or on her skin. I recognized her immediately.

"Kayla?" I asked. Kayla Stevens is another member of our book club. In fact, she lives on the same block as I do. She's a grade behind me.

"It's horrible!" she cried, shaking her head. Then, noticing the door was open, she quickly went over and closed it, peering out the window.

"I don't see any of them," she said.

"Any of who?" Tommy asked. "What happened to Wayne? Are there more kids like him?"

"We've got to lock this door," Kayla said. She sounded terribly frightened.

"Can't," Tommy replied, shaking his head. "You have to have the key to lock it."

"Then, we've got to find a way to barricade the door!" Kayla said frantically. She looked around the room. "We have to keep them out! We can't let any of them come close to us!"

"What are you talking about?" Carlos asked.

"I'll tell you what I know," Kayla said, shooting a nervous glance out the window in the door. "But first, let's put some desks in front of the door so they can't get in."

"Let's use the teacher's desk," Tommy said. "It's heavier."

Carlos and Tommy bolted to the front of the classroom. Each one of them grabbed the opposite ends of the teacher's desk. I moved some of the student desks out of the way to create a path, and they carried the bigger desk across the classroom. Kayla stepped aside as they pushed it up against the door.

"That should do it," Tommy said. "I don't think anyone will be able to get in. Not with that thing pressed against the door. It weighs a ton."

"What in the world is happening?" I asked Kayla.

"You won't believe it," Kayla said, sitting down at a desk. She shook her head. "Not in a million years."

"All we know is that Wayne is really sick, and there are bugs crawling all over him," Carlos said.

"Oh, it's much worse than that," Kayla said. "It all started this afternoon, right after lunch."

We listened as Kayla described the horrible things that had happened, and how things were getting worse with every passing minute.

"First," Kayla began, "you need to know I'm not infected. They haven't got me yet."

"Infected?" I asked. "By what?"

"I'll get to that," she said, pulling aside a lock of blonde hair that had fallen over her face. She was very animated, moving her arms and hands quickly as she spoke. "Let me start at the beginning. During lunch, I noticed that a kid was really sick. I don't know his name, but I've seen him around.

"Anyway," she continued, "when I asked him about it, he said he felt strange. He said something had bitten him earlier—a bug or a spider—and ever since, he had started feeling worse and worse."

"What did he look like?" Tommy asked. "Was his skin all white?"

Kayla shook her head. "Not at first," she replied. "I told him he should see the school nurse right away. Bites from insects or spiders can be serious. My brother was bitten by a spider last year, and we had to take him to the hospital. He got really sick."

"So, what happened?" I asked. "Did he see the school nurse?"

Kayla shrugged. "I don't know. The bell rang, and I had to go back to class. But later, when I was running an errand for my teacher, I saw the same kid. This was just before school let out for the day. He was walking in the hall. Really slow, too, like he was in some sort of trance. He stumbled a few times, and I thought he was going to fall. When I got closer, I could see that his skin had turned white. There were dark rings around his eyes."

"That sounds like Wayne!" Tommy said.

Kayla shook her head. "No," she replied. "It wasn't Wayne. Wayne is in our book club. I don't know who this kid was."

"Did he have bugs on him?" I asked.

Kayla bobbed her head. "I counted four of them, crawling in his hair, on his clothes, on his arm . . . ew!" She shuddered. "It was so gross! I tried to talk to him, but all he did was make growling sounds. Then, he came after me."

"He *attacked* you?" Carlos asked.

"He tried," Kayla said. "But I ran away. I ran to the office, and I told Mrs. Brady, the principal, what happened. All she did was laugh."

"The principal didn't believe you?!?!" I asked.

Kayla shook her head. "She thought I was making the whole thing up. But when I was on my way back to class, I found one of the bugs. It was on the floor, dead, and partly skooshed. I ran to the science lab; found a small, plastic container; and went back to get the bug. I took it to Mr. Ames, the science teacher. He said it was a cootie."

"A what?!?!" Tommy blurted.

"A cootie," Kayla said. "He seemed really interested. He said it's the first cootie he'd seen in a long time. He wanted to know if it had bitten me, and I told him no. I told him about the kid I'd seen in the hallway, though. He said he'd look into the matter in the morning, that cooties are dangerous. Mr. Ames said that if you're bitten by even one cootie, you become infected and turn into a zombie-like human. And the cooties remain on you and continue to feed. I've seen a few kids that are already infected. In fact, most of the members of our book club have been bitten. They're wandering the halls right now!"

If I hadn't seen Wayne—if he hadn't come after us the way he did—I would have never believed Kayla. Her story would have been just too crazy to believe.

But in light of the circumstances, I believed her. As far-fetched as it sounded, as bizarre as it seemed, there was a cootie infestation going on at our school at that very moment.

"What happens to them once they become infected?" I asked. "Do they . . . do they *die?*"

Kayla shook her head. "Mr. Ames didn't say. He just said that it's serious, and that once you become infected, you go crazy, and there is no cure. He said there was an outbreak in Oklahoma City a few years ago, and it was awful. Hundreds of people became infected by cooties."

This is worse than a nightmare, I thought. *This is horrible. This isn't happening on a movie set in Hollywood . . . this is Tulsa, Oklahoma. Things like this aren't supposed to happen.*

"Let's get out of here," Tommy said. "The windows don't open, so we can't get out that way." He stood, leaned around the teacher's desk, and peered through the window in the door.

"See anyone?" I asked.

Tommy shook his head. "There's no one around. We can make it to the front door and get out. Or, maybe there are still some teachers in the office. Maybe Mrs. Brady is still here. She might believe the four of us, since we've all seen the same thing."

"I'm all for getting out of here," I said. "My life is more important than our book club."

"Carlos," Tommy said. "Help me move this desk away from the door."

Carlos got up from the desk where he had been sitting. He and Tommy lifted the desk and moved it aside. Then, Tommy again peered both ways through the window in the door.

"I don't see anyone," he said. "Hang on. I'll make sure there's no one else in the hall."

Tommy grasped the silver doorknob, turned it slowly, and pulled the door open. It didn't make a sound. He took a step forward and cautiously poked

45

his head out, first looking to the left, then to the right. Then, he leaned back into the classroom.

"Not a soul in sight," he whispered. *"Let's get out of here."*

The front doors were only about a hundred feet away, and I figured we'd make the sprint in only a few seconds. In seconds, we would be outside the school, where we could go for help.

That plan was about to change.

9

We lined up behind Tommy, and he gave one last check of the hall to make sure there weren't any infected kids waiting for us.

"I don't see anyone," he said. *"Let's go. Head for the front doors as fast as you can. Now!"*

The four of us took off running, tearing down the hall. From where we were, we couldn't quite see the front doors, but we would in seconds. Beyond, on the opposite side of the hall, the office door was closed, and through the glass wall, I could see that the lights were off. It seemed everyone had gone home for the day, except, of course, Mrs. Candor and Mr. Jones the custodian. But they were nowhere in sight.

We were running as fast as we could, sprinting down the hall. Lockers and classroom doors flew past. Everything was a blur.

Suddenly, from another hall wing, four kids emerged in front of us: Wayne, Chelsea Hillerman, Rick Terrino, and Laura Stilman. All of them are in our book club. Chelsea, Rick, and Laura looked just as hideous as Wayne. Their skin was white; their eyes were sunken and dark. And they all had black cooties crawling on them!

"They must have heard us!" Carlos shouted. "Now they are going to try to stop us!"

It didn't take long to realize that our four classmates had cut us off. They spread out the width of the hall, and I knew there was no way we'd get around without coming into contact with them. Which meant, of course, there was no way we would make it to the front doors.

The four of us skidded to a stop.

"Back the other way!" Tommy shouted. "We can go out the doors at the other end of the building!"

We spun and ran in the opposite direction. I didn't even turn around to see if the four infected kids were coming our way, because I was certain they were. I just ran.

Tommy and Carlos are fast runners, and they passed me and ran ahead a few feet. Carlos's shoes had come untied, and I knew it was only a matter of time before he tripped and fell. Kayla lagged behind a little bit.

But Carlos didn't trip . . . Kayla did. She tripped, stumbled, and fell to the floor, screaming.

I stopped and turned. Tommy and Carlos did the same.

"Kayla!" I shrieked. *"Get up! They're coming! Get up!"*

Kayla scrambled to her feet . . . but she wasn't moving fast enough.

"Hurry!" I screamed. Wayne, Chelsea, Rick, and Laura were getting closer by the second. They were moaning and licking their lips as they approached.

"Kooooo . . . teeeeez," they mumbled.

I knew Kayla wasn't going to make it on her own. If someone didn't help her, she was going to be overtaken by the four infected kids.

So, I did the only thing I could do: I raced to help her. All she needed was a helping hand to pull her along.

The question was this: could I make it to her before Wayne, Chelsea, Rick, and Laura?

Kayla began screaming.

"I twisted my ankle!" she shrieked. *"I twisted my ankle!"*

Still, I thought there was hope. Carlos and Tommy had turned around, and they, too, were racing to Kayla's aid.

It was with numbing horror that I realized we were too late. Wayne, Chelsea, Rick, and Laura had been closer to Kayla than we were, and in the next instant, they pounced on her, knocking her back to the floor and pinning her down. They made horrible moaning sounds while Kayla cried out in pain.

"Leave her!" Tommy shouted. *"We can't do anything for her, now. We've got to focus on getting out of here, or they're going to get us, too!"*

It was horrible to hear Kayla cry out in pain as the four cootie-infected kids attacked her on the floor. But there was nothing I could do. If I tried to help her, they would get me, too. For Kayla, it was already too late.

But for the three of us? We still stood a chance of making it out of the school . . . but we'd have to act fast.

Realizing there was nothing I could do for Kayla, I turned back around and began running down the hall. Tommy and Carlos were running, too. By now, Kayla had stopped screaming. I felt horrible that I hadn't been able to help my friend.

"I can't believe that just happened!" I yelled as I sprinted down the hall. "I can't believe any of this!"

"We'd better believe it!" Carlos replied. "We'd better believe it, if we want to get out of here!"

We ran past the dark office, past classrooms and walls of red lockers. Everything was a blur.

Up ahead, the front doors came into view. I shot a quick glance over my shoulder to see the mob—including Kayla—coming after us. They weren't really running, but they were stumbling along at a fast pace.

Cooties, I thought as I ran. *I never thought they were real. I thought that cooties were just imaginary bugs.*

I remembered what Tommy had said to Brianna earlier in the day, how he'd teased her. She'd bumped into him, and he pretended to brush away imaginary cooties from his arms.

And I remembered what Mr. Ames, the science teacher, had told Kayla: *if you're bitten by even one cootie, you become infected and turn into a zombie-like human. There is no cure.*

It seemed impossible, but we had seen the effects with our own eyes.

There is no cure.

Wayne, Chelsea, Rick, Laura, and now Kayla had all been transformed into horrific, cootie-infected zombies.

There is no cure.

I wondered who else, if anyone, had been bitten and infected.

My answer came soon enough. Ahead of us, two

kids—Alec Ross and Shelby Keller, two more book club members—emerged from a classroom.

They were infected.

Shelby had once been a very pretty, dark haired girl. She was tall and athletic. In fact, she was the best soccer player in school. Her team won the district championship every year, and she always scored the most goals.

Now, however, Shelby was no longer a pretty girl. She had been transformed into a hideous monster, just like the five zombie-kids behind us. Alec, too, was suffering the same effects. His mouth was open, and he was moaning and snarling.

Tommy and Carlos stopped running. I stopped, bumping into Carlos.

Behind us, Wayne, Chelsea, Rick, Laura, and Kayla were coming. Ahead of us were Alec and Shelby, blocking the front doors.

Our only escape.

We'd been ambushed . . . and there was no way out.

Our situation seemed hopeless.

We'd managed to put some distance between us and the five kids coming after us, but we'd been headed off by Alec and Shelby, who were, at the moment, much closer . . . and getting closer by the second.

"We'll have to try to dodge them," Tommy said. "There's only two of them, and there's three of us. We'll have to try to distract them, and maybe we can slip around without coming in contact."

"Good thinking," Carlos said. "Besides . . . they can't get all three of us."

I didn't like that thought, either.

If they can't get all three of us, I wondered, *which one or two of us would they get?*

Either way, we'd have to make a decision fast. Both groups of zombie-kids were getting closer.

Tommy darted to the side of the hall and stood next to a locker.

"Carlos!" he said. "Get over on the other side. Tricia! Stay in the middle. Use your best football moves to dodge them!"

"But I don't play football!" I said.

"Just do your best!" Tommy replied.

I shot a glance over my shoulder. Wayne, Chelsea, Rick, Laura, and Kayla were still stumbling toward us, but they were a few classrooms away.

I looked at Alec and Shelby, and I hoped that I was quicker than they were. By now, they were only twenty feet from us.

Shelby came straight at me. However, Tommy leapt from the side of the hall, waving his arms.

"Here, Shelby!" he shouted. "Get me! Get me!"

The tactic worked. He diverted Shelby's attention, and she turned to go after him. Alec was on the other side of the hall, heading for Carlos. That left a big open space right in the middle of the hall.

It was the opportunity I needed. I ran straight ahead, past Alec and Shelby. I ran until I reached a classroom, then I turned around.

Tommy had spun back to the side of the hall and had bolted ahead of Shelby. He was now running toward me. Carlos had done the same, although he had been lucky. Alec had nearly been able to wrap his arms around him. Still, Carlos had managed to slip away, and he, too, was now running toward me.

"The doors!" Tommy shouted, pointing as he ran. "Head for the doors!"

I ran. Tommy and Carlos were on my heels, and the hoard of zombie-kids—seven of them, now—had ganged up and were still coming for us.

But we were faster. We were faster, and we were closer to the doors. I saw the glowing red EXIT sign, and a surge of hope welled up inside me.

We've made it! I thought. *There's no way they can catch up to us.*

Or, maybe they could.

You see, there was one little detail we hadn't thought about. A little detail that quickly became a *big* problem.

There were two exit doors, side by side, at this end of the building. Both doors have horizontal metal bars that, when pressed, allow the door to be pushed open.

I was the first to the doors. I couldn't wait to feel the fresh air on my face, to smell the outdoors, to run as fast as I could away from the school. There were houses all over the place, and I'm sure we could quickly find someone to help us.

But when I pressed the bar and pushed, nothing happened! The door wouldn't open!

"Go!" Tommy shouted from behind me.

"I can't!" I replied in frantic frustration as I

pushed the bar again. "The door won't open!"

I tried the other one. Tommy and Carlos arrived at my side, out of breath, huffing and puffing. They, too, tried the bars. No luck.

"Oh, man!" Carlos said. "You know what? Mr. Jones locks all the doors when school lets out for the day! The doors are locked from both the inside and the outside! That's why Mrs. Candor has her own key, so she can let us out after book club."

The mob of cootie-infected kids—all seven of them—were still coming toward us.

"Okay," Tommy said. "Let's think quick." He looked up and down the hall, then pointed. "Into that classroom over there," he said.

"But we might just be backing ourselves into a corner," I protested. "If we get into that classroom and they get in, there will be nowhere we can go."

"In case you haven't noticed," Carlos replied, "we don't have a choice. That classroom is the only place we can go."

Tommy was already darting across the hall. Carlos and I followed.

And, amazingly, our luck changed.

"There's a bolt lock on this door!" Tommy

exclaimed as he slammed it closed. Just above the doorknob was a small, oval-shaped knob, no bigger than a quarter. Tommy turned it, and there was a loud *ker-clunk* as the deadbolt sank into place.

"That'll hold off those bug-infested monsters," Tommy said.

"They're not monsters," I said. "They're our friends. They're just sick."

"Yeah," Carlos said. "But like Mr. Ames told Kayla: there's no cure. They're only going to get sicker. Maybe they'll—"

Carlos was interrupted by a shuddering thunder as Wayne and Rick slammed into the door, followed by Chelsea and Alec. Their white faces were pressed against the window. The sudden attack surprised the three of us, and we leapt back from the door.

But the lock held. The door shook as they tried to get it open, but they were unsuccessful.

"Go away, you buggy freaks!" Tommy shouted. "You're not infecting us, too!"

When the zombie-kids realized they weren't going to be able to get us, they backed away from the door. Their faces looked empty, lifeless. Their eyes were ice cold, and the dark rings around them made them look even more menacing. They looked like they were dressed up for Halloween.

But Halloween was a long ways off. This was April . . . October was six months away.

Finally, they walked away. We could no longer see them through the window in the door. Which, of course, didn't mean our ordeal was over. We were safe—at least for the time being.

"Now what?" Carlos asked.

"I don't know," Tommy said, shaking his head. "But we're safer in here than we are in the hall. Here, in the classroom, they won't be able to get at us. Maybe we should just wait. Sooner or later, our parents are going to wonder where we are. They'll come looking for us."

"But that might not be for hours," Carlos said. "What about the window?"

The three of us looked over at the large glass window on the other side of the classroom.

"It doesn't open," Tommy said, shaking his head. "Most of the windows in the classrooms don't open, and the ones that do are too small to climb through."

"Yeah," Carlos said. "But if we can find an open

window, we could yell for help. Someone might hear us and call the police."

Suddenly, I got an idea. It was a good one, too. Normally, I would have never thought of doing it in a million years. But now, things were different. We were fighting to save our lives. And when I told Carlos and Tommy what we would have to do, they agreed: my idea just might work.

My idea?

"Let's smash the window," I said.

Carlos gasped. Tommy raised his eyebrows.

"Man, we could get in a lot of trouble if we do that," Tommy said.

"In case you haven't noticed," I said, "we're in a lot of trouble already."

"But it's against the law," Carlos said.

I couldn't disagree with Carlos. Sure, it was breaking the law. Sure, we could get into a lot of trouble. I heard about some kids at another school in Tulsa who smashed some windows with bricks. They were arrested, were kicked out of school for the rest of the year, and had to pay for the damage.

Our situation, though, was much different. Those kids had smashed the school windows for no reason. We, on the other hand, were trying to escape. We were trying to save our lives. In light of that, if we explained it to the school, our parents, and the police, they would have to understand: we had no other choice but to break the window in order to escape and save our lives.

"I guess we don't have any other option," Tommy said. "I'm with you, Tricia. I say we smash the window and get out of here."

"What are we going to break the window with?" Carlos asked, looking around the classroom. "I don't see anything heavy and solid."

We searched the room, but we didn't find anything. There was a football in a basket in the corner, but that wouldn't work. It was too soft.

Then, I looked at the numerous desks arranged in rows.

Of course, I thought, mentally rolling my eyes.

"Hey," I said, putting both hands on a desk. "These are pretty heavy. Let's use a desk."

"Great idea!" Tommy said. "Come on, Carlos. You and I can do it."

Tommy and Carlos grabbed the nearest desk and hauled it to the window.

"Ready?" Tommy asked.

"Let's go for it," Carlos replied.

I covered my ears. I knew the sound of shattering glass wasn't going to be very loud, but the very fact that we were about to smash a school window made me nervous. I didn't like what I was about to see and hear.

Tommy and Carlos heaved the heavy desk at the window. It crashed into the glass . . . and bounced off!

"Wow," Tommy said. "That glass is strong. Let's try it again."

Again, Tommy and Carlos tried to smash the window with the desk. Again, the desk just bounced off harmlessly. There wasn't even a scratch on the glass.

"You know what?" Carlos said. "I'll bet it's shatterproof glass. It won't break, no matter what."

"Let's try one more time," Tommy said. "Use every muscle you've got."

Nope. Once again, the desk bounced off the

glass and fell sideways to the floor.

"Well," I said, "I *thought* it was a good idea."

"It was a *great* idea," Tommy said as he righted the desk. "And it would have worked, if it was normal glass."

"At least we're safe here, in the classroom," Carlos said. He sat in one of the student desks.

"There's still something we can do," Tommy said. He looked at the door.

"What's that?" I asked.

"We can try to make it to the office," he said. "If we can make it to the office, we can use a phone to call for help."

"We should have thought about that before," Carlos said, "when we ran right past it."

"But we didn't know the exit doors were locked," I said. "Had we known the exit doors wouldn't open, we probably *would* have went into the office."

"I'll check it out," Tommy said. "Wait here."

He walked to the door and peered out the window. Then, he turned the small knob above the doorknob, and there was a loud *click* as the bolt slid back into the door. He pulled the door open slowly, and peeked outside.

"Nobody around," he whispered.

"Wait a minute," I said. I walked to the door and looked at Tommy. "What if they're in the office? Or in one of the classrooms? They could be waiting for us, right now."

Tommy scratched his head. "I hadn't thought of that," he said.

After thinking for a moment, he spoke.

"Okay," he said. "Here's what we'll do. I'll go to the office by myself. You two stay here. If I see anyone, or if they come after me, I'll come back. Keep your eye out for me so you can let me back in. If you see the crazy kids, close the door and lock it."

While I didn't like the idea of Tommy going alone, I realized that it was probably the smartest thing to do. The office wasn't far away, and if he could make it there and use the phone, he'd be able to call for help.

"Be careful," I said. "You don't know where they might be."

Again, Tommy leaned forward and peered up and down the hall.

Carlos got up from the desk and joined us at the door. "Yeah," he said to Tommy. "Be cool."

Tommy managed a grin and a wink. *"Cool as*

butter," he whispered. *"Okay. I'm on my way."*

And with that, Tommy left the classroom and vanished around the corner.

Carlos and I leaned forward and watched. Tommy wasn't running; rather, he was making a great effort to be perfectly silent. He took big strides, but his sneakers made no sound as he made his way down the hall toward the office. His head turned, and he peered into classrooms as he passed them, on the lookout for our infected classmates.

"He's going to make it," I whispered. *"He's halfway there already."*

We continued watching, and I felt a huge wave of relief when Tommy finally made it to the office and vanished.

"He's there!" Carlos said. "He made it!"

Seconds ticked by. One minute. Then two. We watched, waiting for Tommy to emerge, but also looking for any sign of the cootie-infected book club members.

"I'm sure he's had time to use the phone and call for help by now," I said.

"He's probably talking to the police at this very second," said Carlos.

We waited. When three minutes had gone by, I began to get nervous.

When four minutes had gone by, I began to get worried.

And when I saw seven figures emerge from a classroom farther down the hall, I became horrified.

They were heading for the main office!

"*What do we do?*" Carlos whispered. Both of us remained at the classroom door, our noses poked around the corner, each of us peering down the hall with a single eye. We were far enough away and hidden enough so that I didn't think the kids could see us.

"*There's nothing we can do,*" I said quietly. "*There are seven of them, and only two of us.*"

My heart sank. Tommy would be cornered in the office. There was nowhere for him to go, and there was no way he'd be able to fight off seven cootie-infected kids.

I felt terrible. Tommy was a good friend. Now, he was going to become infected. Then, he would join the others and come after Carlos and me. It was an awful, awful feeling.

Of course, I'd never been in a situation like this before. I'd never been so scared.

Then, I made a decision: we were getting out of school. Some way, somehow. I was not going to give up. We were going to escape. There simply *had* to be a way out. There *had* to be.

Think. Think. Think.

While my mind spun, trying to think of a way out, we gazed in horror down the hall. Stumbling as they walked, we watched the seven kids enter the office like deranged robots.

Think.

"Okay," I whispered to Carlos. *"This is our chance to get out of here for good, while they're in the office."*

"What are you talking about?" Carlos whispered back.

"See those yellow doors down there?" I said, nodding.

"The doors to the auditorium?" he replied. *"What*

about them?"

"Number one," I replied quietly, *"they're always unlocked. Number two, there's an emergency exit behind the stage. Maybe that door will be unlocked. Even if it's not, there are plenty of hiding places behind the stage or in the prop room. But we have to hurry. There's no telling when they're going to come out of the office. And Tommy will probably have become one of them, so that will make eight."*

"Why don't we just stay here?" Carlos asked. "We could just stay here and lock the door."

"Because," I whispered, *"sooner or later, they'll find a way to get in. And we're not going to get out of here if we just stay put."*

"Then, let's go," Carlos said. "Let's go now, before they come out of the office."

Quickly, we slipped out of the classroom and sneaked down the hall. I opened the auditorium door, and we stole inside . . . not realizing we were about to make one *huge* mistake.

15

Getting into the auditorium was easy. Oh, I was really nervous as we tiptoed down the hall. Horrified, actually. But we made it to the doors of the auditorium and were able to slip inside without anyone seeing us.

Inside the auditorium, it was very, very dark. There were only a few small safety lights burning on the wall, providing just enough glow to see the aisles. Which was a good thing for us, because it meant that it would be easier to hide, if we needed to.

"Let's go down by the stage," I said.

"There's an emergency exit, right over there," Carlos said as we began walking down the carpeted aisle. "It's on the other side of the auditorium."

"Yeah," I replied, "but it opens up into the hallway. But I've been backstage, and I think there's an emergency exit there. I think the door opens up outside, at the back of the school."

While we walked, I began wondering a few things. *Where was Mrs. Candor? Where was Mr. Jones, the custodian?* Nothing was making any sense. *Had they been infected, too? Was it possible that they, too, had become like zombies? Were they wandering the halls, just like the kids in the book club?*

And I couldn't stop thinking about Tommy. There was no doubt that he, too, was now infected. I was certain that he'd been attacked just like Kayla had been. Tommy had been a good friend . . . now, he was just like all of the other cootie-infected kids.

Carlos and I made it to the stage. It was even darker here and nearly impossible to see anything.

"The steps are over there," I said, "on the other side of the stage. We can climb onto the stage and crawl under the curtain."

"I'll follow you," Carlos said. "I can't even see my shoes."

"Just go slow, and be careful so you don't trip,"

I replied.

We're getting out of here, I told myself. *We are going to find a way out. Some way, somehow.*

I just kept telling myself that, over and over, as we made our way through the inky darkness in front of the stage.

Some way, somehow.

"Okay," I said. I stopped. "The stairs are right around here somewhere."

"It sure would help to have some light," Carlos said. "It's really, really dark."

Carlos was about to get his wish. A faint glow bloomed from behind us. Startled, we both turned.

The light came from the auditorium door. It was now open, and stale light from the hallway poured inside.

Suddenly, the auditorium lights came on. By this time, our eyes had adjusted to the darkness, and the harsh light caused us to squint.

Even so, we could clearly see the back of the auditorium. We could see rows and rows of empty seats. We could see the bright, burning lights. We could see light pouring in from the hallway.

And we could clearly see the small mob of

cootie-infected kids as they poured through the open door and began walking down the aisle, heading for us.

16

"The stage!" I said as I quickly found the steps and took them two at a time. It was much easier to see with the lights on, but that also meant the attacking hoard could see us, too.

Carlos was right behind me as I reached the stage, dropped to the floor, and rolled under the curtain. Here, it was very, very dark, except for the light bleeding through the outer edges of the curtain.

"Grab my hand!" I hissed to Carlos as we stood. "It's going to be even darker when we make our way behind the stage. But that's where the emergency exit is."

Carlos found my hand and gripped it tightly. We

made our way to the back of the darkened stage. All the while, we could hear the groaning and sneering of the infected kids coming from the auditorium as they made their way down the aisle.

And every time I began thinking about how hopeless our situation was, I pushed the thought away and replaced it. I replaced it with: *we're getting out of here. Some way, somehow. We're getting out of here.*

I wasn't sure if I believed it myself, but I refused to admit defeat.

However, as we stumbled around the back of the stage, we didn't find the familiar *EXIT* sign glowing red. I was almost certain there should have been one behind the stage, but there wasn't.

"Where's the door?" Carlos whispered.

"I don't know," I replied. *"I was sure I'd seen one back here."*

"If we don't find a way out, we have to find a place to hide!" Carlos hissed. *"Those guys are going to be on the stage at any second."*

Carlos was right, of course. I had been wrong about the emergency exit. Now, we were backstage, and there was no way out.

"The prop room is around here somewhere," I

replied. *"But it's going to be hard to find in the dark. Come on!"*

"What's a prop room?" Carlos asked.

"It's a place where they store things the actors and actresses use during plays and performances," I replied. *"Costumes, chairs . . . things like that."*

Carlos was still gripping my hand tightly as we stumbled and fumbled our way around backstage. In the auditorium, the moaning and snarling had grown louder. I knew we had seconds—mere *seconds*—to find the prop room or find some other place to hide.

I bumped into a wall and found a doorknob. At the same time, I heard footsteps on the stage stairs.

I turned the knob, opened the door, and stepped inside. Carlos was still holding my hand, and he followed behind. Quickly, I pulled the door closed, and I began to fumble in the darkness, looking for a light switch. I found one, and flipped it up.

A single bulb in the middle of the room blossomed.

It was the prop room!

Looking around, there were all kinds of things that were used in plays: chairs, tables, wooden swords and muskets, racks and racks of clothing, all cluttered in the tiny room. There was much more to see, but I didn't want to take the time. I wanted to find someplace to hide.

"Let's hide behind the clothes racks," Carlos said.

"No," I replied. "That's too obvious. They'll find us, for sure."

On the other side of the room, there was a huge pile of clothing on the floor. If I ever let a pile of clothing get that big in my bedroom, Mom would have grounded me until I was grandma's age.

But in that pile, I saw hope. It was easily big enough for Carlos and me to burrow into. We could dig into the pile and be completely hidden. Hopefully, the zombie-kids wouldn't find us. It wasn't the *best* place to hide, but it seemed like the only chance we had.

"See that pile of clothing over there?" I said, pointing.

"Yeah," Carlos answered.

"We're going to climb in and bury ourselves. But here's the trick: I've got to turn off the light. If they open the door and see the light on, they'll know for sure that we're hiding in here, somewhere. They'll search until they

find us. If we turn the light off and hide, maybe they won't discover us."

Beyond the door, I could hear the muffled sounds of feet scraping across the stage, along with that awful, continuous moaning. They were getting closer by the second.

"Okay," Carlos said.

I turned off the light, and the world seemed to vanish. There wasn't a single pinpoint of light anywhere. I might as well have had my eyes closed.

We waded cautiously across the room, totally blind, maneuvering around the places where I thought a chair or table might be. Once, I bumped into something, but I was going slowly and didn't make any noise.

When I found the place where I thought the pile of clothing was, I knelt down and felt around with my hands.

"I found it!" I whispered. *"It's right here. Crawl in and pull a bunch of clothing on top of you."*

We both burrowed into the pile of clothing like chipmunks. The fabric smelled old and musky, but I hardly noticed. Nor did I care. All I wanted to do was hide.

When I was sure I was buried beneath the mound of clothing, I stopped. Carlos, too, had stopped moving.

Were we hidden? I couldn't tell, of course.

We were about to find out. I heard the doorknob jiggle. Then, I heard a light creaking sound. The door was opening.

Then, the light clicked on. Although I was buried in clothing, I could still see faint angles of light in and around the clothing piled around me.

I heard shuffling feet. They drew closer.

Closer.

I closed my eyes. I bit my lip.

Please don't find us, I thought. In my mind, I could see a white face appearing as the clothing around me was pulled away. I could see dark circles around menacing eyes. I could see those awful, black cooties leaping onto my skin . . . .

And when the footsteps stopped at the pile of clothing where Carlos and I were hiding, I knew that, for us, it was the end of the line.

I was so freaked out that I almost burst from my hiding place. Where I would go or what I would do after that, I didn't know. I knew I'd get infected by cooties, just like the other members of the book club. But it was maddening, hiding in the pile of clothing, waiting to be discovered. Waiting to see if, by some slim possibility, we wouldn't be discovered. It was an awful, gut-churning feeling. I had no idea how intelligent the infected kids were. Were they like the zombies I'd seen on television? Those weren't very smart at all. They were more like mindless robots, searching for food.

Maybe that's what cooties do to you, I thought.

Maybe, if you get infected, you become mindless and have no control over what you're doing.

Regardless, it was a horrifying feeling to know that one of the cootie-infected kids was, at that very moment, only a couple of feet away.

But as the seconds flew by like hummingbirds, I grew hopeful. No hand reached into the pile of clothing to drag me out. No pasty white face leered at me. In fact, I heard footsteps again, and this time, they moved away.

Whoever it was, they were walking away! They hadn't discovered us!

I held my breath as the footsteps shuffled across the room. I heard things being moved around. Someone, obviously, was searching for us. They were lifting things up, pushing things around. I could hear them going through the racks of clothing, and I was glad we weren't hiding there.

Then, I heard another set of feet enter the room. There was more banging around, more shuffling of items. More moaning, more snarling. I thought I could make out whispering, but I wasn't sure.

Soon, the footsteps moved farther away. The light clicked off, and the door closed.

I heaved a muffled sigh of relief through the clothing. I could still hear the sounds of scuffling feet and soft moaning beyond the door, but I was now sure that we wouldn't be discovered. We might have to stay in the pile of clothing for a while, but I was sure that, once the zombie-kids thought we weren't hiding backstage, they would leave.

All of those thoughts went out the window when Carlos let out a loud sneeze.

Carlos's sneeze caught me by surprise, and I flinched. Then, a rush of terror swept through my body like a hurricane.

Carlos just sneezed! I thought. *Of all the rotten, lousy luck! Had the zombie-kids heard it? Would we be found out?*

I knew Carlos hadn't meant to sneeze. In fact, I couldn't blame him. With all of the clothing piled on top of us, there was bound to be some dust or something that would bring on a sneeze from either one of us.

I waited for the door to open and the light to

come on. I prepared myself for the worst.

But no one came.

If anything, the sounds of the cootie-infected kids were now farther away. Soon, I was convinced that they hadn't heard Carlos sneeze. The pile of clothing surrounding him had probably been enough to muffle the sound. The door to the prop room was closed, of course, and that had helped. If Carlos had sneezed when one of them was in the prop room, it would've been a different story altogether.

"Sorry about that," Carlos whispered.

"Don't worry about it," I whispered back. *"I'm just glad they didn't find us."*

"What do we do now?" he asked.

I thought for a moment. *"Let's just wait here,"* I replied. *"We're safe for the moment. Let's try to come up with a plan to get out of the school."*

Thoughts whirled through my head like a swarm of bees. I knew there *must* be a way out of our school. Where was it?

Then again, I also knew that Mr. Jones locked all of the doors from the inside, once school got out. That meant that no one got in . . . and no one got out, unless they had a key.

And where was Mr. Jones? I figured he'd be busy mopping the floor or emptying trash or whatever it was that custodians did after school.

That, I figured, was our best shot. Find Mr. Jones. If we found him, we'd find his keys—keys that would unlock the doors. It was a good plan, I thought. I knew it would be difficult, and maybe a little dangerous . . . especially with so many cootie-infected kids roaming the halls like hungry monsters.

Still, we had to take the chance. Find Mr. Jones, find the keys.

It sounded simple.

It wasn't going to be.

19

I don't know how long we waited in that giant pile of clothing. Probably at least ten minutes.

Finally, after I was pretty sure it was safe to come out of hiding, I started pushing clothing off of me.

"Carlos," I said, "come on out. I think they're gone."

I stood. Of course, I still couldn't see anything, because the light wasn't on. Slowly and cautiously, I made my way through the room, feeling my way through the darkness. Three times, I bumped into things, but I was being careful and didn't knock anything over or trip and fall. That would be the *last* thing I needed.

"Where are you?" Carlos asked.

"I'm right here," I replied. *"I'm trying to find the light switch."*

Finally, I found it. I turned the light on and squinted in the stinging light.

Carlos was standing on the other side of the prop room, in front of the pile of clothing, which was now in more disarray than it had been.

"Now what?" he asked.

I told him my thoughts about Mr. Jones, and how I thought that if we could only find him, he could help us.

"But what if he's one of them?" Carlos whispered.

"I thought about that," I said. *"If that's the case, there's nothing we can do about it. But if we can find his keys, we can let ourselves out."*

Carlos walked across the room and stood next to me. *"Hey, whatever you think is best,"* he said quietly. *"I just want to get out of here alive."*

I looked around the room, and I couldn't believe our luck. On a shelf was a flashlight! I reached for it and clicked it on. A bright beam of light shot out like a white laser.

"This will come in handy," I said. "It's going to be dark backstage."

I turned off the flashlight, then I reached out and flipped the light switch off. The room was plunged into darkness once again. I found the doorknob and slowly pulled the door open, listening for sounds. I heard nothing.

But the backstage area was very dark. It was difficult to make out anything. I could see a few shapes here and there, but not much else.

Satisfied that we weren't going to be ambushed by a bunch of crazed kids, I switched on the flashlight. A spindle of light lanced through the inky darkness.

"Follow me," I said, and I walked out the door. Carlos followed, and we carefully made our way around backstage . . . until we found something I had never seen before.

Something I never knew existed.

Something that was about to change *everything*.

I was thankful I'd found the flashlight, as it was much easier to see where we were going. There were a lot of things we could have bumped into. Plus, now that we had a light, we could search the area backstage to see if there was another way out.

"What's that over there?" Carlos asked, pointing to the far side of the stage.

I shined the light to where he was pointing and walked quietly in that direction. The beam of light illuminated cables that rose to the top of the stage like wiry snakes. Above, dozens of light cans were poised, waiting in silence for the next big show, when they would come alive in an explosion of dazzling colors.

There was also a large, square board—a piece of electrical equipment—that had dozens of tiny dials and buttons. I figured it was probably used to control the lights and the sound. Whoever was in charge of that must really know what they were doing.

"Is that what you saw?" I asked, shining the light on the equipment.

"Yeah," Carlos said. "But from back there, the shadows made it look like a door."

I shined the light around, but I didn't see an exit.

"Let's try farther back behind the stage," I said. "With a flashlight, it'll be easier to see."

"Why don't we just find some lights and turn them on?" Carlos asked.

"No," I said. "If anyone comes into the auditorium, they'll see the lights and know we're back here. We're safer with the flashlight. If we hear anyone, I can shut it off, and we can hide."

We strode farther backstage and poked around. We found several dressing rooms and a large, walk-in closet with racks and racks of clothing.

It was there, in the closet, that we also found

something else.

Carlos was the first to spot it. He pointed to the floor. "What's that?" he asked.

I trained the flashlight beam on the floor, but I didn't see anything unusual . . . at first.

"What's what?" I asked, sweeping the beam across the floor. Shadows bent and leapt.

"Right there," he said, and he took the light from my hand and trained the beam on a spot a few feet away.

Something shined. A handle of some sort, flush with the wood floor.

"Look at that," Carlos said, sweeping the beam along a dark, thin crevice that made a large rectangle in the floor of the closet. It was about the size of a bathtub. "This isn't a floor," he said. "It's a trap door of some sort." He moved the light to another spot on the floor. "See? There are hinges, right there. This is some kind of trap door."

A trap door? I thought. *In a closet? That's strange. Unless—*

"It probably just leads to a storage room beneath the stage," I said.

"We won't know unless we open it," Carlos said.

101

He handed the light back to me and walked into the closet. Leaning down, he grasped the handle and pulled. It was heavy, and I helped him lift it up. He stood on one side, and I stood on the other, and we raised the door until it was straight up in the air.

"Lean it back a little bit more," I said. "There's a chain fastened to the door and the bottom of the floor. It will keep the door from falling backward."

As we leaned the door back farther, the chain tightened, and we were able to let go of it.

I pointed the light down.

"Holy smokes," I breathed. *"I can't believe it!"*

21

I'd expected to find a small storage space—something only a few feet deep—beneath the floor. What we found was something altogether different.

Steps.

A wood staircase led down to—

Where?

The walls were made of old brick, and the air smelled dry and thick.

"Where does *this* go?" Carlos asked.

"You've got me," I replied. "I never knew it was here."

"Maybe it goes to a cellar," Carlos said.

"A cellar?" I replied. "In a school?" It sounded strange. I imagine some schools might have basements, but who ever heard of a school with a cellar? That didn't make sense.

"Those steps look old," Carlos said. "It looks like it's been here a long time."

"But our school isn't that old," I said. "This is really, really weird. I wonder what's down there?"

I moved the beam of light back and forth, but the only thing we could see were the steps and the walls on either side.

"Let's find out," Carlos said. "It might lead to a way out."

While I didn't think so, I figured we might as well check it out. One thing I *was* sure of: there were no zombie-kids down there.

Carlos's shoelaces had come undone. He knelt down to tie them, then stood.

The steps were wide enough to allow us to walk down, side by side. We moved slowly, and I must admit, I was a little afraid. It was eerie, sinking down into the floor beneath the stage.

The wood steps creaked beneath our feet. Step by step we went, and I moved the beam back and forth. The bricks were the color of beach sand, held together by a reddish-brown mortar.

"There," I said, training the beam of light ahead and down. "There's the floor, right there."

We took another step, and another. As we drew closer to the floor, we could see it better. The floor looked to be sand, or hard packed dirt.

Another step, and another.

Creak.

Walking side by side with Carlos made me feel better. Safer.

The problem was that, in doing so, we were *both* putting our weight on each step at the same time. The wooden steps were old. One of them was far too weak to support both of us.

Creak . . . .

With no warning at all, the board we stepped on snapped and broke in two, plunging us through the stairs!

22

Two things prevented us from getting hurt badly: the stairs and the sand floor.

When the step broke, Carlos and I plunged straight down. However, the space we fell through was thin—only as wide as the step. Our fall was broken when our arms hit the next step, which also snapped, but it slowed our plunge a little. The flashlight was knocked from my hand and went out. Thankfully, we fell only a couple of feet, and we landed on the sand floor like two sacks of potatoes.

Then:

Silence and darkness.

I was on my back. My right leg and my left knee ached, but not badly.

"Are you all right?" Carlos asked.

"I think so," I replied. "I guess that wasn't very smart of us."

"Hey, we didn't know," Carlos replied. I heard him move. "Where's the flashlight?"

"It got knocked out of my hand when my arm hit the step," I said. "It's got to be around here somewhere. I hope it's not broken. Are you okay?"

"I'm fine," Carlos said. "We got really lucky, that time."

The air was dry, and our fall had kicked up dust. It tickled my nostrils, and I sneezed.

It didn't take long to locate the flashlight, as it was only a few feet from where we'd landed. Thankfully, when I clicked it on, it worked. The beam was full and pronounced, illuminating the dust in the air like a cloud of smoke.

Ahead and above us was the staircase. There was a brick wall behind us and brick walls on both sides.

"This isn't good," Carlos said. "We're trapped. There's no way out."

"I'll bet there is," I said.

"How?"

I shined the light on the bottom of the stairs, sweeping it back and forth. "The steps are weak," I said. "The wood is old and rotting. That's why that step broke, and we fell through. I'll bet we can break some of these steps and get out."

I was right. We got to work pushing and pulling at each step, discovering that much of the wood was rotten. The decay made it easier to break the boards. Soon, we had pulled enough of the stairs apart to step through.

I shined the light ahead of us. We were in a large, tunnel-like hallway. It was about eight feet wide, but the ceiling seemed low. Lower than the ceiling in our house. If I reached up, I could touch it. And there was no floor . . . just sand.

"Where does this thing go?" I said. "I never knew there was anything like this here."

"I bet no one does," Carlos said.

We started walking. I shined the flashlight beam back and forth. We hadn't gone more than twenty feet, when I saw something.

"Up there," I said, aiming the flashlight beam.

"There's a room or something, on the left."

We kept walking until we reached the opening. There was no door. It was just a dark room . . . until I shined the light inside.

Carlos leapt back. I almost screamed.

In the room, on the sandy floor, was a human skeleton!

23

Seeing the bony, decaying skeleton took my breath away . . . until I realized what I was looking at. Then, I almost laughed out loud.

"It's not real," I said. I knelt down and tapped the skull, and it gave off a hollow sound. "It's made of plastic. It's just a prop, used in theater. Look around."

I shined the light around the room. There were numerous other stage props: mannequins dressed in old clothing; boxes with writing on them; an old, torn theater curtain with a thick curtain rope attached to it; several racks of ratty clothing; and a few empty, metal racks that were bent and kinked.

"It's all just junk," Carlos said.

"Someone must have tossed all this stuff here years ago," I said. "Maybe they weren't using it anymore."

"The skeleton sure freaked me out," Carlos said. "I'm glad it's not real."

We left the room and continued down the corridor. Cobwebs hung down in many places, and I had to sweep some of them away to keep them out of my hair and face. We came across several more rooms, but they were small and empty. None of them had doors.

"We'd better find another way out of here," Carlos said. "Being that we busted up the stairs back there, we won't be able to use them."

I hadn't thought of that. In breaking the wooden steps, we'd destroyed the stairs . . . and our way out.

But I was certain there must be some other exit, and I hoped it led outside. We just had to find it.

We continued walking slowly, warily. It seemed strange that we were actually walking *beneath* the school.

And, while we walked, I thought about our situation. I felt bad for my friends in the book club.

What would happen to them? Would they get better? Was a case of the cooties like a cold or flu, that would pass with time? Or was it much worse? Mr. Ames had told Kayla that there was no cure. What if they—

Knock it off, Tricia, I reminded myself. *Remember what you told yourself: somehow, some way, you're getting out of here.*

Then, I thought about Tommy again. He had been a great friend, and I was going to miss him.

Still, maybe he'd been able to use the phone. Maybe help was already on the way. Maybe the outside of the school was swarming with police and emergency vehicles at this very moment.

"Hey," Carlos said, bringing my thoughts back to where we were. "What's that, up there?"

His arm shot out, and I shined the light where he was pointing.

"I told you!" I said. "I knew it!"

Ahead of us, on the right, was a door. Like the stairs, it was made of wood, and it was old and weathered. There was a dusty brass knob about waist high.

"Maybe it opens to the outside," Carlos said.

"Only one way to find out," I replied. "Come

113

on."

We hustled up to the door. I grabbed the doorknob, turned it, and pulled. It had only opened about an inch when Carlos leapt back . . . and screamed.

24

Carlos's shriek was enough to cause me to let go of the knob and jump back, but I didn't know what had frightened him.

"What?" I asked. I looked at the door and tried to peer through the crack, but it was too dark. "What did you see?"

"Right there!" Carlos replied. "Shine your light up there!"

He was pointing to a spot on the door, above our heads. I raised the flashlight beam. There, hanging from the ceiling on a fine, shimmering thread, was a spider. He was no bigger than a dime, but the way

Carlos had screamed, I would have thought it would have been the size of a cat.

"Are you kidding me?" I asked. "You *really* got freaked out by a spider *that* small?"

"Hey, I don't like spiders," Carlos mumbled. "I don't care how big they are. And that one almost got me."

I shook my head as I grasped the doorknob again. I opened the door, and the flashlight beam illuminated another staircase, ten steps in all. These steps, however, were made out of the same brick as the walls, and they rose up to a door. Even from where we stood, it was obvious the door was made of metal and was much newer. It was dark blue, and the doorknob was made of steel.

"That's our way out of here," I said. "Follow me."

I strode through the doorway and took the steps two at a time. Carlos was right behind me. I grabbed the doorknob. It was cool and smooth.

"Wait," Carlos said. "Don't open it yet."

"Why not?" I asked.

"Because we don't know where it leads," he replied. "It might lead outside, but it might lead back into the school. If so, we have to be careful."

He had a good point. If the door opened up into a school hallway and the zombie-kids were around, we'd be in trouble.

"I'll open it just a little," I said. "Just enough to see where we are."

Slowly, I turned the knob and pushed the door. It opened a tiny bit, enough for me to see a thin band of darkness; nothing else. I pushed the door open farther and poked the flashlight beam inside.

"Hey!" I whispered. *"I know where we are."* I pushed the door all the way open and stepped into the dark room. Carlos followed.

"This is Mr. Jones's office!" I said, sweeping the beam of light around the room. Shadows ducked and jumped as the light illuminated a mop, several large garbage cans, a shelf stocked with cleaning supplies, a chair, and a desk that was cluttered with papers. In fact, the entire office was in disarray. Nothing seemed to be in order. Our custodian did a nice job keeping the school clean, but his office was a mess.

I swept the beam of light over the desk and along the wall.

"What are you looking for?" Carlos asked.

"A phone," I said. "If there's a phone in here, we can call for help."

No luck. I figured that, since Mr. Jones carried a walkie-talkie with him, he probably didn't need to have a phone in his office.

I continued moving the beam along the wall, until I saw something shiny glistening in the bright beam. It was right next to the main door that opened into the school hallway.

I stared. It took a moment for me to realize what I was looking at. Then, when I took a step closer to the glimmering, tiny objects, I knew what it was: a set of keys.

Keys!

"That's what we need!" I exclaimed. "Keys! Now we can unlock the font doors and get out of here!"

"Yes!" Carlos said, throwing his fist into the air. "We're going home!"

Finally—*finally*—things were starting to look up. After what had happened, after everything we'd been through up until that point, I didn't think we'd stand a chance of getting out. Oh, I *told* myself we would, but I wasn't sure if I actually *believed* myself. Of course, we'd still have to be careful. The group of infected kids could be anywhere, and we'd have to make sure we didn't attract their attention. But now that we had keys, I knew we'd finally be able to get out. We were mere minutes away from freedom and safety.

And we would have been, too, if I had paid closer attention to something very important . . . .

25

I snapped the wad of keys off the wall and held them up. "These are our ticket out of here," I said proudly. "Ready to go home?"

"I was ready to go home an hour ago," Carlos said.

I walked over to the door that would open into the hallway.

"The main doors are going to be down the hall and to the left," I said to Carlos. "But first, let's make sure no one is around. Open the door and peek out."

Carlos turned the knob and slowly opened the door. Light poured in through the thin seam. The lights

121

were off, but there was still daylight coming through the windows.

Keeping the door cracked only an inch or so, Carlos leaned forward and peered out.

"I don't see anyone in that direction," he whispered. Then, he slowly pushed the door open farther and stuck his head out, checking the other direction.

"Nobody that way, either," he said.

"Then, let's head for the front doors," I replied. I shut off the flashlight and put it on Mr. Jones's desk. We wouldn't be needing it anymore.

Carlos slipped out the door, and I was right behind him. With the way our luck had been going, I expected to see the mob of infected kids pour out of a room and swarm after us. Thankfully, I saw no one.

Carlos and I ran down the hall as fast as we dared, trying to be as quiet as we could. We didn't want our shoes slapping the floor and making noise, as that might attract the attention of the cootie-infected zombie-kids.

Up ahead, I could see the front doors, and I realized that, finally, we were going to get out. We had the keys, and there wasn't a single kid in sight.

Until we passed the office.

Carlos and I had been so focused on getting to the front door that we weren't paying attention to the rooms as we sped past. As we sprinted by the office, a sudden motion gave me only a split-second to respond.

By then, it was too late.

One of the infected kids had spotted us first, and he burst out of the office door. There was nothing Carlos and I could do. The attacker hit Carlos and me at the same time, and we were sent careening across the hall and tumbling to the floor.

26

It happened so fast that I couldn't tell who or what had hit me. The impact of the attack knocked the keys from my hand, and they went flying. Wildly off balance, I hit the floor. I rolled and, luckily, didn't get hurt. Carlos, too, went down, and he gave out a heavy grunt when he hit the hard tile. There was a metallic *ching!* as the keys hit a locker and another *ching!* as they fell to the floor.

In a panic, I rolled sideways and stood, ready to run. Carlos was on his feet, too, and we were about to take off running again . . . until I saw who was also on the floor.

Tommy!

His skin looked normal, his eyes didn't have dark rings around them.

"It's you!" I shouted, not sure whether I was happy or scared. After all, if he'd been infected by cooties, that meant that he would be just like the other kids in the book club.

"Are you guys all right?" Tommy asked, getting to his feet. "I thought something happened to you."

"We're fine," Carlos replied. His shoelaces had come loose, and he quickly tied them. "We thought something happened to *you*. We saw everyone go into the office right after you. We thought they got you."

"I hid under a desk," he said. "They didn't find me. I've been hiding there all this time. I had just decided to make a run for it, and I accidentally ran into you. I didn't even see you coming. Where have you guys been?"

Carlos began to speak. "We've been—"

I interrupted him. "We'll tell you later," I replied. I snapped up the wad of keys on the floor. "The important thing is that we've found Mr. Jones's keys. We can unlock the doors. Let's get out of here, and we'll talk later."

"Sounds good to me," Tommy said.

The three of us hurried to the front doors.

Now, I thought, *which key is it?* There were at least a dozen keys on the key ring. Some were gold, some were silver. Some were thin, some were wide.

I tried one.

Nope.

I tried another.

Not that one, either.

I tried another one. And another. Then another. Some didn't even fit, others fit but wouldn't turn.

"What's the matter?" Carlos asked. He sounded frantic.

"I can't find the right one!" I replied in frustration. I tried another key.

Nope.

Of course, I had no way of knowing it, but *none* of the keys would work. You see, I had taken Mr. Jones's *personal* keys . . . keys to his house, car, things like that. None of the keys I had were going to unlock the school doors.

It was a problem that became even bigger when we heard a noise in the hall. The three of us turned.

"Oh, no," Carlos whispered.

The mob of infected kids had discovered us. Altogether, I counted nine: Wayne, Chelsea, Rick, Laura, Kayla, Alec, Shelby, and two new kids, Jacob Stearn and Mia Reeves. That meant everyone in our book club—except us, of course, and Mrs. Candor—had been infected by cooties.

All nine were coming toward us, stumbling, trance-like. Their arms were outstretched, their eyes were dark, and their mouths were open.

The front doors were still locked.

The keys didn't work.

I was exhausted, and I didn't think I could run anymore. This whole thing had been going on since school let out. That was over an hour ago. And yet, it felt like days. It felt like days had passed since Tommy and Carlos and I had been walking down the hall, talking, on our way to the library for book club.

I no longer had the strength to fight. I no longer had the energy to run. I was so tired of everything. I had to face the fact that there was no way out, that we were trapped in our school, and we were going to become just like the rest of the kids in our book club: infected by cooties.

But Carlos had been thinking.

"Wait a minute," he said. Lines appeared on his forehead, and he looked deep in thought.

"That's it!" he suddenly blurted. "I think I know where we can go to be safe! A place where they can't get us!"

I sure hoped he was right.

27

"Back into Mr. Jones's office!" he shouted. "Think about it: we can lock ourselves in his office! They won't be able to get to us!"

He was right! I'd forgotten that the custodian's door locked from the inside. That meant anyone on the other side—in the hall—would have to use a key. Without it, they wouldn't be able to get in!

Carlos had already started running down the hall, and I followed. Tommy ran right alongside me, and the three of us darted into Mr. Jones's office. Carlos flicked a light switch, slammed the door, and turned the lock.

Suddenly, we heard pounding and slapping at the door. We could hear the kids moaning, and some of them were speaking.

"*Let . . . us . . . in,*" someone mumbled, but it was so unnatural sounding, so *animalistic,* that I couldn't tell who it was.

We backed away from the door. There was a space of about a quarter of an inch from the floor to the door, and I could see shadows moving about. They were moaning and snarling. Someone was saying '*kooo-teeez*' over and over. Someone tried to reach beneath the door with their fingers, but the space was too small.

"Now what?" I asked.

"Nothing," Carlos said. "We're stuck in here, but it's a lot safer than being in the hall. Here, they can't get to us."

After a few minutes, when the zombie-kids realized they couldn't get to us, they left.

I breathed a sigh of relief. We were safe, at least for the time being. Yes, there wasn't anyplace for us to go. However, considering the fact that the infected kids couldn't get to us, being locked in the custodian's office wasn't all that bad.

We explained to Tommy about the secret basement we'd discovered.

"It's right here," Carlos said, and he walked across the room and opened the door on the opposite side. Tommy peered down at the brick walls and staircase.

"Those bricks look old," Tommy said. "It looks like this basement has been here for a long time. A lot longer than our school has. Is there another way out?"

I shook my head. "We didn't find any. There is a room with a lot of old theater things. Junk, mostly. Other than that, there wasn't anything else. No other doors, anyway." I told him about the staircase we'd found beneath the trap door in the closet floor in the backstage area of the theater, and how it had collapsed. I explained how we had to destroy the staircase to get out.

"And we found this," I said as I picked up the flashlight from Mr. Jones's desk. "It was in the prop room backstage. It came in handy."

"Well, we're safe here," Tommy said, looking around Mr. Jones's office. "At least for the time being. Man . . . he sure is messy."

Then, we heard something.

Footsteps.

Heavy footsteps. They stopped at the custodian's door, and we heard keys jingling, and a key was inserted into the lock.

"Mr. Jones!" Carlos said. "He's back!"

Oh, Mr. Jones had returned, all right . . . but when the door opened, and we took one look at him, we knew he wasn't there to help us.

28

I had hoped that Mr. Jones hadn't been infected. He would have known what to do and would have helped us. We all might have been able to get out of the school.

But when the door opened, and we saw him standing there, we knew it was too late. His face was white, just like our friends that had become infected. His eyes had dark rings around them, and just like the zombie-kids, he had several cooties on his arms and shoulders. Mr. Jones is bald, and he had a cootie on the very top of his shiny head.

He groaned, snarled, and raised his arms. He

looked like a bald Frankenstein with a bug on his head.

There was only one place we could go: through the doorway that led downstairs into the old basement. Still, that wouldn't prevent him from coming after us, but what else could we do? Mr. Jones was blocking the door, and there was no way we would be able to overpower him.

Tommy and Carlos were thinking the exact same thing, as they had already started toward the door on the other side of the office. I followed. Carlos threw open the door and the three of us raced down the stairs, two steps at a time. I was lucky that I still had the flashlight in my hands, and I turned it on. The beam illuminated the dark, gloomy hall.

"This way!" I cried, which was really sort of pointless. There was no other way we could go!

But we could try to hide. I thought maybe if we put some distance between Mr. Jones and us, we could hide in the room where we'd found the junk storage. It was a long shot . . . but it was all we had.

It seemed to take forever to find the room. I knew it was only a matter of seconds, but when you're trying to outrun a cootie-infected custodian, it seemed like time dragged on and on.

Finally, we found the room and ducked inside.

"Find a place to hide!" I hissed.

The three of us scurried around the room, looking for anything we could hide behind or beneath. I found three boxes piled on top of each other, and I crawled behind them. All the while, I kept the flashlight on so that Tommy and Carlos could find a place.

Tommy found an old tarp made of plastic, and he knelt in the corner and pulled it over his head. Carlos hid behind a rack of old clothing.

I shut off the flashlight, and we waited. My heart beat thick and heavy, keeping time with every passing second. I listened for Mr. Jones, but it seemed my heart was thrashing so loudly that I couldn't hear anything else.

One minute went by, then another. Another. We didn't hear anything. I kept waiting to hear the sound of jangling keys, indicating that Mr. Jones was getting closer, but I didn't hear anything.

That didn't mean that he wasn't looking for us. Maybe he was just being quiet, trying to draw us out of hiding. After all: I was sure he was well aware of the basement and probably knew there was no place for us to go.

But maybe he doesn't, I suddenly thought. *Mr. Jones probably doesn't know that we destroyed the staircase. He probably thinks that's where we were heading! If he was after us, he wouldn't follow us into the basement . . . he would go to the backstage area and wait for us to come up the stairs and into the closet!*

None of us had said a word for some time. I was the first to speak.

"I think it's safe to come out," I said. "I don't think he's coming after us." I explained to Tommy and Carlos that, if Mr. Jones was smart, he'd head for the backstage area and the closet, not knowing that we'd demolished the stairs and couldn't get out. Just the same, he wouldn't be able to get to us, either.

"We have to outsmart him," Tommy said.

"We have to outsmart *all* of them," I said. "The question is, how?"

Confident that Mr. Jones hadn't followed us, I turned on the flashlight and stood. Tommy and Carlos came out of hiding, and the three of us stood together in the middle of the room.

"The three of us have to be smarter than those freaks," Tommy said.

"They're not freaks," I replied. "They're our friends. They're just sick. They're infected."

"But Mr. Ames said that there is no cure," Carlos said. "They aren't going to get better. In fact, they're probably just going to get worse."

Suddenly, Tommy let out a shriek that was so loud, my ears hurt.

"Oh my gosh!" he wailed, pointing down. *"What's that?!?!"*

Although Tommy's shriek startled me, when I saw what he was pointing at, I laughed out loud.

It was the fake human skeleton!

He hadn't seen it when we first entered the room because we were in too much of a hurry to find places to hide.

"Don't worry," I said, training the beam on the plastic bones. "It's not real. It's just a stage prop."

Tommy let out a sigh that sounded like a blast of steam. "Wow," he said. "That thing looks real. I'd like to have that in front of our house for Halloween."

"Yeah," Carlos agreed. "It fooled us the first

time we saw it, too."

"Guys," I said, "we really have to think of a way out. Here, we're sitting ducks. There is nowhere for us to get out of this basement, except through Mr. Jones's office. And we don't know if he's in there or not."

"Let's have a look at the stairs," Tommy said. "Maybe there's something we can rig up."

"We'll have a look," I said, "but let's go quietly and be careful. They might be waiting for us."

"But," Carlos said, "if they can't come down and we can't go up, we don't have to worry."

I shook my head. "If Mr. Jones realizes we're down here, and that the only way out is through his office, he'll know we're trapped. We already know he's been infected. Maybe he's working with the other kids, now. Maybe they're all on the same team."

"A team of zombies," Carlos said. "It sounds like a bad movie."

"Well," Tommy said, "it's a bad movie that won't have a happy ending for us, unless we can get out of here. We've got to figure something out."

"Come on," I said, walking out of the room and into the corridor. "Let's go have a look at the broken staircase."

Silently, we trundled down the dark hallway, dodging cobwebs that hung from the ceiling. Soon, the flashlight beam lit upon the pile of broken steps.

"You guys really did a number on that thing," Tommy said.

"It was pretty old," Carlos said. "We were lucky we weren't hurt. We could have easily broken a bone, or a rusty nail could have punctured our skin."

That's when I heard a noise from above. Not loud, just a soft scratch. Quickly, I aimed the beam upward . . . and into the faces of six zombie-kids, glaring down at us.

30

Despite the horror that swept through my body, I was thankful that we'd destroyed the stairs. As it was, the zombie-kids couldn't get to us. Even though they were only a few feet above us, there was no way they could get into the basement unless they jumped . . . in which case, they'd probably break a bone or two.

I swung the flashlight beam across their faces. I saw Wayne, Chelsea, Alec, Brianna, Rick, and Kayla. They didn't even look like my friends anymore. Just empty husks of what they once were.

Tommy, Carlos, and I took a step backward. The zombie-kids were directly above us, and I was worried that one of those cootie bugs would fall off one of the them and land on us.

Then, they were gone in a flurry of scuffling and shuffling feet . . . and I knew exactly what they were going to do. They were going to race down the hall and into Mr. Jones's office. From there, they would be able to enter the basement. We'd be trapped, helpless.

"They're going to come after us!" Carlos shouted. "They're going to come in through the custodian's office because they know there's no other way out. We're trapped!"

"No, we're not," Tommy said. "Tricia . . . give me your flashlight."

I held out the light, and Tommy snapped it from my hands. "Stay here, and be ready!" he ordered.

"Ready for what?" I asked. But Tommy had already started off. He ran down the dark hall. All we could see was the white beam frantically bobbing back and forth.

"What's he doing?!?!" Carlos asked.

Without a light, I could no longer see Carlos. "I don't know," I replied.

Suddenly, the light vanished. It looked like

146

Tommy had gone back into the room where the old stage props were.

"I hope he knows what he's doing," Carlos said.

"I hope he hurries," I said.

Suddenly, the light reappeared. Tommy raced back to us.

"Here's the light!" he said to me. "Shine it up!"

"Up where?" I asked.

"Up there, up there!" he ordered.

I shined the light up through the entryway where the staircase had once stood. It was then that I caught a glimpse of something looped on his shoulder.

It was the rope that had been attached to the old, torn curtain in the stage prop room!

Then, I realized what Tommy was going to do. He was going to use the rope to climb out of the basement!

"Keep the light up there while I tie a loop," Tommy ordered as he pulled the coil of rope from his shoulder. His hands worked quickly as he tied a noose at the end of the rope.

"That should do it," he said. "Hold the light steady. I have to toss the rope up there and find something solid to hook this loop to."

The only thing I could see that might possibly work was the doorknob of the closet door. The door was open, and the knob was in plain view. Had the door been closed, we wouldn't have seen it.

Tommy held the noose in his right hand and tossed it into the air. It came close to the knob, but the loop just bounced off the door and fell back to our feet. Tommy picked it up and tried again.

"Hurry," I said. "It's not going to be long before they come after us down here."

"I'm trying," Tommy said. He tossed the rope, missed again, and tossed it once more. This time, the loop caught around the doorknob. Tommy pulled it tight. The door moved, but the loop held around the knob. Tommy gave it a heavy tug.

"That'll work," he said.

Then, we heard a distant noise.

A door opening, and a shuffling of feet on steps.

Then: moaning.

Snarling.

The zombie-kids were in the basement and were headed our way.

31

Once he'd secured the rope to the doorknob, Tommy wasted no time. He leapt into the air, grabbed the rope, and pulled himself up like a monkey. I was really surprised at how fast he climbed. In seconds, he had pulled himself out and was standing above us, in the closet.

And one thing that horrified me as I was watching him: I knew there was no way I was going to be able to pull myself up. I wasn't strong enough.

Meanwhile, I could hear the infected kids coming. I shined the light down the hall, but I didn't see them. Still, I could hear them, and I knew time was running out.

"Tricia!" Tommy yelled. *"Climb up!"*

"I'll never be able to do it!" I replied. *"I'm not strong enough!"*

"Carlos!" Tommy said. *"Go! Tricia . . . when Carlos gets up here, you grab the rope and we'll pull you up!"*

I liked that plan much better . . . but would we have enough time? It was a good thing the infected kids didn't move as fast as normal kids; otherwise, they would already have been upon us.

Carlos climbed the rope. He wasn't as fast as Tommy, but he made it. As soon as he did, I tossed the flashlight up. Carlos snapped it out of the air and set it down on the floor. I grabbed the rope.

"Hang on tight!" Tommy ordered. *"Pull with me, Carlos!"*

I felt myself being lifted off the ground. Down the brick hallway, I heard the zombie-kids getting closer.

"Hurry!" I shrieked. *"They're almost here!"*

Inch by inch, Tommy and Carlos pulled.

Halfway there.

Behind and below me, I caught a glimpse of a

shadow. And another.

"They're almost here!" I wailed. *"Pull!"*

With a single heave, Tommy and Carlos yanked me higher. By now, my shoulders were level with the floor in the closet. I let go of the rope with one hand and placed it on the floor, hoping to be able to use my upper body strength to help pull me the rest of the way out.

But it wasn't to be. Before I could do anything more, I heard snarling and growling from beneath me. A hand grabbed my left foot. Another grabbed my right foot.

"Kooo . . . teeez," one of them snarled in a gravelly, low voice. *"Kooo . . . teeez . . . ."*

Tommy and Carlos had been strong enough to pull me up . . . but there was no way they'd be able to pull me from the clutches of the infected zombie-kids.

I screamed and screamed, waiting for Carlos and Tommy to lose their grips, waiting to be pulled down into the basement to meet a fate worse than death.

32

"*Hang on!*" Tommy shouted. "*Don't let go!*"

He held my left wrist with both of his hands; Carlos held my right with both of his. Beneath me, the ravenous, zombie-kids had hold of my feet. It was hard to believe that, only a few hours ago, they were my friends. Now, they had become deranged lunatics, made crazy by the effects of the cootie infection.

Tommy and Carlos pulled. I kicked and kicked. Suddenly, both of my shoes came off . . . and I was free. Tommy and Carlos pulled me up and out of the stairwell, falling backward and banging into the door. I fell to the floor and bumped my knee. I winced in pain, but I shook it off. A bumped knee was a lot better than being pulled, kicking and screaming, into the basement by the gang of zombie-kids.

Oh, how I wished this wasn't happening. I wished we were in the media center, talking and laughing, discussing the book we were reading, and eating chocolate chip cookies. I wished—

Wait a minute! I thought. *That's it!*

"To the media center!" I said. "If we can make it there, we can lock ourselves in! They won't be able to get us! If we hurry, we can make it before they get out of the basement!"

"We should have thought about that an hour ago!" Tommy said.

"We didn't know then what we know now," I replied. "Come on! We don't have much time!"

We raced through the darkened backstage area, finally reaching the stairs. It was uncomfortable, running without my shoes, but I didn't let it bother me. I was just glad Tommy and Carlos had been able to pull me up from the basement.

We ran to the other side of the theater, up the aisle, and stopped at the double doors beneath the glowing *EXIT* sign. By this time, we were out of breath, panting and wheezing. I pushed the bar, and the door opened.

"Careful," Tommy said.

I poked my head out and looked both ways, up and down the darkened hall.

"Nobody!" I hissed. "Let's go!"

I pushed the door open and the three of us burst into the hallway. Tommy's and Carlos's shoes slapped the floor as we ran, and my socks slipped and slid on the tile.

As we ran, I kept my attention ahead of us. I kept expecting someone to leap from a classroom and cut us off, but no one did.

Finally, the media center came into view. It, too, was dark, and all I could see inside were shadows.

We're going to make it, I thought. Then, in the next moment, I thought: *no, we're not. Something bad will happen, and we won't make it to the safety of the media center. The way our luck has been, something bad will happen.*

But nothing did. The three of us raced to the front door of the media center. Tommy pulled the door open, and we darted inside. I flipped on the light while Tommy locked the door. Carlos raced across the library to the other side to lock the back door. When I heard both locks click into place, it was music to my ears.

We made it, I thought. *We're safe.*

Then, we sat at a table in the middle of the library, where we could look out the windows on both sides and see into the hallways.

"Finally," I said. "We're finally safe. Nobody can get to us."

"Not unless they have a key," Tommy said.

"Yeah," Carlos said. "Speaking of which: where is Mrs. Candor? We haven't seen her anywhere."

Tommy began to speak. "Maybe she's—"

"Wait!" I interrupted. "What's that?"

We listened. I was sure I'd heard something, like the distant sound of metal jingling.

Suddenly, a figure appeared in the hall, and we heard the distinct sound of keys rattling.

"It's Mrs. Candor!" I said. "She's finally here! She'll know what to do!"

We heard the sound of a key entering the lock, and the door opened. Mrs. Candor came through the door, and things suddenly went from bad . . . to worse.

33

When Mrs. Candor saw us, she stopped. We looked at her, she looked at us. She seemed surprised to see us; we were just as surprised to see what she looked like.

She had been infected.

Like the others, her face was all white. Dark rings circled her eyes, and there was a nasty, red scar on her cheek. Even from across the library, I could see a few black cooties on her arm. There were two or three in her hair.

And while it was obvious she was surprised to see us, she didn't seem all that threatening . . . for a moment. Then, she dropped her keys on a table and raised her arms. Her eyes widened, and her mouth opened. She snarled and began stumbling toward us.

"The back door!" Tommy shrieked.

"I'm getting really tired of this!" Carlos shouted as the three of us leapt from our chairs and ran across the library.

"I was tired of this a long time ago!" I replied as we darted around tables and bookshelves.

We reached the back doors, only to find we had company. In the hall, the infected kids appeared. They tried the door, found it locked, and began slapping at the windows. It was a horrifying sight to see our friends—monsters, now—pressing their faces against the glass, moaning and snarling like wild animals.

I turned around. Mrs. Candor was still coming toward us.

"Circle around her!" I said. "The library is big enough, and we can get around her and get out through the front door!"

I ran to the left, Carlos ran to the right, and Tommy followed me. Mrs. Candor came after us, but she had to go around tables and bookshelves. Tommy and I were faster than she was, and we were easily able to make our way through the library to the front door.

And at the last moment, I did something that I knew would save us. On the table, near the doors, was Mrs. Candor's set of keys. I knew for a fact that she had a key that would unlock the school doors.

Quickly, I grabbed the keys from the table. Carlos opened the library door, and the three of us tumbled over one another as we burst into the hallway.

"To the front door!" I shrieked. *"I have Mrs. Candor's keys! We can finally get out of here!"*

"We'd better hurry!" Tommy said. *"Those kids are going to circle around and come after us! Mrs. Candor, too!"*

We raced down the hall toward the front doors of the school. I had a hard time running, because my socks were slippery on the tile.

Behind us, we could hear the mob of infected kids coming our way, but I knew there was no way they'd be able to catch up to us.

But there *was* someone who could catch up to us. By then, we'd forgotten all about him, until he suddenly emerged from his office.

Mr. Jones.

He didn't come toward us. Instead, he stumbled across the hall and stood by the front doors, blocking our exit. He stood with his feet apart, his arms crossed. He was ready for anything.

We stopped running. Behind us, the hoard of zombie-kids was coming.

Once again, we were trapped.

34

We stood in the middle of the hall, gasping for breath. Our heads turned back to look at the mob descending upon us from the hallway, then back to Mr. Jones, standing in front of the door. I knew there was no way we'd be able to get out . . . not with him standing in our way. With any luck, we'd be able to get past him and escape down the hall. But there was no way he was going to let us go out through those doors.

But then what? Sooner or later, we were going to run out of options. There weren't too many places we could go, and it was only a matter of time before they caught up to us. Then, we'd become infected ourselves.

Still, I wasn't ready to give up yet. Neither were Tommy and Carlos.

I was just about ready to make a run for it when Mr. Jones's office door opened. Chelsea, Wayne, and Rick emerged, stumbling into the hall. They were coming toward us.

I shot a panicky glance over my shoulder. The other group was still coming, and they were only about fifty feet away. I snapped around to face Chelsea, Wayne, and Rick.

"We're in for it, now," Carlos said. "I don't think we're getting away this time."

Carlos was right. I kept looking back and forth, up and down the hall, trying to think of a plan, trying to think of a way out. There were no classrooms nearby, nowhere to hide where we could be safe. There was nothing around that we could use to defend ourselves.

Wayne began to growl and show his teeth. Chelsea began mumbling and snarling. Soon, everyone—including Mr. Jones—was making loud, animal-like sounds. They sounded more like ravenous beasts than humans.

It was then I realized that, truly, it was finally the end of the line for us. As the hoard approached from behind, and Wayne, Chelsea, and Rick came at us from the other direction, I realized that this time, there was no escape, no way out. Oh, I would fight as best I could, but it was pointless to try and run.

Closer and closer they came, until they had surrounded us in a wide circle. It was a wall of white faces, dark eyes, and hungry mouths. Tommy, Carlos, and I stood in the middle, our backs to each other, looking in horror at our infected, zombie-like classmates.

There was a moment of eerie silence. Then, as if an unseen signal had been given, the group attacked, swarming all over us, knocking us to the floor.

35

I screamed, doubled my right hand into a fist, and swung. I didn't even aim, as there really was no time. My hand connected with something hard, and I heard someone squeal. A boy.

"Ouch!" he cried. "Hey, knock it off! That hurt!"

Then: laughter. The group of zombie-kids took a step back. More laughter, and more. Tommy, Carlos, and I were on the floor, looking up in shock and confusion.

"Surprise," Kayla said. "April Fool's!"

"Wh . . . what?" I stammered. "April Fool's?"

"It's April Fool's day," Wayne said.

"Yeah," said Brianna. She looked at Tommy. "I wanted to get you back for what you said to me this morning," she said.

"Huh?" Tommy replied.

"Cooties," Brianna said. "Don't you remember? When I accidentally bumped into you, you said I had cooties."

"Oh, yeah," Tommy said. "I was only joking."

"We were, too," Brianna said. "We just thought it would be a good April Fool's joke to get you back."

"And it worked!" Rick piped.

"But what about the cooties?" I asked, pointing. I could clearly see bugs in everyone's hair. Kayla had one on her forehead.

"These?" Wayne said, pulling a bug from his hair. "They're just plastic. Some little kid brought a bag of them to school, and he said we could borrow them."

"We used double-sided tape to stick them to our skin," Alec said. He stepped forward and plucked one of the black bugs from his arm, showing me the tape on the bottom side of the plastic insect.

"You . . . you mean this whole thing was a *joke?*" Carlos stammered.

"Yep!" Brianna replied. "Even Mrs. Candor and

Mr. Jones were in on it."

"We used make-up to paint our faces," Shelby said. "It didn't take long at all."

I still had a lot of questions, and I couldn't believe the whole thing had been a joke.

"Even Mrs. Candor?" I asked.

Chelsea nodded. "She helped us make up our faces. It was her idea to use the double-sided tape to stick the bugs to our skin."

"I can't believe this was all a joke," Tommy said.

"It was the perfect April Fool's prank," Brianna said.

"What about the secret basement we found?" Carlos asked.

"That's no secret at all," Mr. Jones replied. It was the first time he'd spoken. "Actually, that basement has been there for a long, long time. It was built in 1918, when the school and the auditorium were first constructed. When the building was completely renovated in 1976, everything was torn down, except the foundation. The new school and auditorium were built on the existing foundation."

"We were lucky we didn't get hurt on those old stairs," I said.

Mr. Jones nodded. "Yes, you were. In fact, I'm going to close that trap door in the closet and put a lock on it, so something like that doesn't happen again."

Farther down the hall, Mrs. Candor appeared. "Come on, everyone," she said. "We've got to get book club started, or we'll run out of time. Get cleaned up and let's get going. We're already an hour behind."

Wayne and Rick helped me to my feet. Carlos and Tommy stood up on their own.

Kayla had been standing behind Wayne, and she stepped forward. She was carrying my sneakers.

"Here you are," she said. "You'll be needing these."

"Thanks," I said, taking my shoes from her. "So, you made up that whole story about the cooties and Mr. Ames?"

Kayla smiled and nodded. "I did a good job, huh?" she said.

I shook my head. "Wow," I said as I put my sneakers on. "You guys sure had us fooled. We really thought you were sick. I really thought that you'd all been bitten by cooties."

"That was the whole point," Rick said. "If you

didn't think we were actually sick, then you wouldn't have been fooled."

"Cooties," Tommy smirked. "We should have known."

While everyone else went into the restrooms to wash their make-up off, Tommy, Carlos, and I continued on to the library. Mr. Jones went into his office.

"I can't believe this whole thing was just a joke," Carlos said as he opened the library door.

"You have to admit," I said, "it was pretty good. They thought it out and really fooled us."

"I'm just glad we didn't break that window with the desk," Tommy said. "We would have gotten into big trouble."

"Oh, wow," I said. "I forgot about that. It's a good thing we didn't break the window, after all. We would have really got into trouble."

Soon, the entire book club was gathered in the library. We talked about the book we were reading, but everyone wanted to talk more about cooties and the prank they had played on us. Mrs. Candor put out a tray of chocolate chip cookies, and they were delicious.

Later, after I said good-bye to everyone and started walking home, I went back over the events of the afternoon. I wasn't mad or anything. In thinking about it, our friends had done a really good job of fooling us. Now, knowing what I did, I could look back and laugh. In fact, I was actually laughing out loud when a dark figure sprang from the bushes and knocked me to the grass.

36

At first, I was sure it was one of my friends playing another prank on me. It was, after all, April Fool's Day. But when I rolled over on the grass, I was shocked to see that my attacker was someone I didn't recognize. That freaked me out.

He, too, seemed shocked. It was a boy. He looked to be about my age. His eyes were wide, and his mouth was open.

"You're . . . you're not Jillian," he stammered.

"No," I said, "I'm not. Who are you?"

"I'm Jason Burke," he replied. "I thought you were my sister. Sorry about that."

"Do you always jump out of the bushes and tackle your sister?" I asked, a little annoyed.

"No," Jason replied. "But it's April Fool's day. What's April Fool's day without a good prank?"

"Tell me about it," I said, remembering what we'd just went through at school.

"Sorry about that," Jason replied, getting to his feet. He reached down and helped me up.

"That's okay," I said. "I'm a little jittery anyway, after what just happened at school."

"What happened?" he asked.

I told him all about the book club, and how our friends had played a joke on us, leading us to believe there was a cootie infestation at the school.

"That would have freaked me out," he said. "But not as much as what just happened to me in Kentucky."

"What happened to you in Kentucky?" I asked. "Is that where you're from?"

Jason nodded. "Yes, and no. I was born here in Oklahoma, but we moved to Kentucky a couple of years ago when Mom got transferred. She used to work for a company that moved her around a lot. Then, she started her own business. We just moved to

Tulsa, because most of our relatives are here."

"But what happened to you in Kentucky?" I asked. "Did someone play a joke on you, like my friends did today?"

"Not hardly," Jason replied. "What happened to us was no joke. In fact, I'm lucky to be alive."

I was really intrigued. "What happened?" I asked.

"To make a long story short," Jason said, "my friends and I were attacked by Komodo dragons. Do you know what they are?"

"I think so," I replied. "Aren't they some sort of big lizard?"

Jason nodded. "You got that right," he said. "But these weren't just any Komodo dragons. These things were *monsters.*"

My eyes widened. "Really?" I said. "I didn't even know Komodo dragons lived in Kentucky."

Jason nodded. "Yep," he said. "But there's a lot more to it than that. Come on. I've got to find my sister. I'll tell you what happened to us as we walk."

We headed down the sidewalk, and all I could do was listen in disbelief as Jason told me his incredible story . . . .

Next:

#27: Kentucky Komodo Dragons

Continue on for a FREE preview!

1

"Are you ready yet?" I called out down the hall. My sister, Jillian, was *still* in her room. We had planned on going for a hike in the woods, but she couldn't decide what shirt to wear. She kept changing from one shirt to another. If she kept it up, we'd *never* get out of the house.

"Just a second, Jason," she said from behind her closed bedroom door.

"You said that ten minutes ago," I said impatiently.

"Hold your horses," Jillian replied.

I sighed. "I'll be on the back porch. We don't

have all day, you know."

"No, you don't," Mom called out from her office. "Make sure you're home by noon."

Mom works out of our house in what used to be a guest bedroom. When she started her own business, she turned it into an office. And she stays pretty busy, because her phone is always ringing, and she's always tapping away at her computer.

I strode across the living room to her office door. Mom sat at her desk, in front of a computer monitor. She had a telephone headset on so she could talk to customers and leave her hands free to type.

"We will, Mom," I said.

Mom smiled. "And stay out of the mud today," she warned.

I smiled meekly and rolled my eyes. The last time I'd gone hiking, it was after a rain. I wound up getting all muddy near a small pond. Mom wasn't very happy when I got home, all soaked and dirty.

Jillian came out of her bedroom. She wore blue jeans and a bright red T-shirt, the color of a fire extinguisher. It had a colorful unicorn on the front.

"That's the same shirt you had on ten minutes ago," I said.

"I decided I liked it best," she said smartly.

I frowned and shook my head. "See ya, Mom," I said, backing away from her office door.

"Bye, Mom," Jillian said.

"Have fun," Mom replied, just as her phone rang. "Don't forget: be home for lunch."

"We will," I said.

Jillian and I walked across the living room, through the kitchen, and out the back door, where we were greeted by a wave of heat. We live in Paducah, Kentucky, which is a city on the western side of the state. It was July, which is month that gets pretty hot in Kentucky. Just to the north of us is the Ohio River and the state of Illinois. It's kind of weird to think that if we drove just a few miles, we would be in an entirely different state.

And where we live is really cool. There are several other homes on Creekview Drive, and behind our house is a big forest. Jillian and I have built a bunch of forts in the woods. Once in a while, Katrina Holland joins us. She lives a few houses away, and she and my sister are best friends.

However, there's an old story that, somewhere in the woods behind our house, is an old, forgotten graveyard. It's supposed to be overgrown with trees and weeds, and it's hard to find. In fact, no one has found it for years. There is only one picture of it, and it hangs at the Paducah Historical Museum. Jillian and I have looked for the graveyard a lot, but we've never found it. Still, there's always a chance that we might, so we go exploring often. That, of course, was our reason for our hike that day: we've always wanted to find the graveyard.

But so far? No luck. There are trails that criss-cross through the woods, but we've never found the graveyard. And we don't always follow the trails. Sometimes, we head into the woods to explore on our own.

What's really cool is that on our hikes, we see all sorts of animals we don't see in the city. Possums, raccoons, deer, skunks, squirrels, rabbits, and all kinds of birds. The forest behind our house is like one gigantic park, just for us.

But today, we were going to find something that should never have existed. Certainly not in Kentucky, or even in the United States, for that matter.

We strode across the back yard and entered the woods. Above, the sun hung like a lemony ball of fire in front of a blue curtain. It was going to be another hot day, that was for sure.

We had hiked for about five minutes when Jillian suddenly stopped. She was looking ahead, trying to peer around trees. We were walking on a trail, and the terrain around us was thick with trees and shrubs.

"What?" I asked, wiping a thin film of sweat from my forehead. "What did you see? A deer?"

"No," she said. "It was smaller." She pointed. "It's in that tree, right over there. But it's not a bird."

I tilted my head to the side, trying to see what she had spotted. I didn't see anything besides trees and branches.

"Probably just a squirrel," I said. "Let's keep going."

We continued on. Branches and tall grass licked at our pant legs like snake tongues.

And, when we reached the tree Jillian had pointed to, we heard a noise. It startled us, and we stopped and looked up.

Jillian shrieked.

I gasped and jumped back.

Looking down at us . . . was a monster.

2

Now, when I say monster, I mean *monster*. Not a monster like Godzilla or anything. What we were seeing was much smaller.

But it was a monster . . . of *some* sort.

He was about eighteen inches long, and, most obviously, some sort of lizard. His skin was leathery, speckled with green, brown, and black markings. His eyes were menacing and sinister, with black pupils ringed with gold. His claws were long and curled, and I was sure they were razor sharp.

And he was hissing at us! His mouth was open,

and we could see his teeth—tiny, but very, very sharp—and a tongue that lashed out like a whip.

Jillian took another step back. "What in the world is that?" she asked.

"It's what you look like in the morning," I replied.

"It's what you look like all the time," Jillian snapped back. "But, really . . . what *is* that thing?"

"I don't know," I replied. "Some sort of lizard, I guess."

"We don't have lizards that big around here," she said. "All we have are those little tiny ones that jet around like little rockets with four legs."

"And those other striped ones," I replied. "I think they're called 'skinks.'"

We continued staring at the lizard-monster in the tree. Although we were much bigger than he was, he didn't seem the least bit afraid of us. In fact, he looked like he was mad, like he was protecting his tree. He certainly didn't look like he was going to run away from us, like most lizards did.

"It must be some sort of rare, endangered species," Jillian said. "I wish we had a camera."

"Maybe he was someone's pet that got away," I

said.

"Or," Jillian said, "maybe he escaped from a zoo. Lots of zoos have lizards."

"Or even a pet store," I replied. "We should check the pet stores to see if any of them are missing a lizard."

We were sure there was a logical explanation as to where the creature came from. A lost pet, a zoo, or a pet store seemed . . . well . . . *logical.*

The truth of the matter was far stranger—and scary—than we could have ever imagined.

We stared at the strange lizard as he watched us from the tree. Actually, *watched* isn't the right word. It seemed like he was *threatening* us, more than anything. He was only about as long as my arm, but he looked like he could prove he was mighty, too. Even though we were a lot bigger than he was, I wasn't sure I wanted to pick a fight with him.

"Let's leave him alone," I said. "We can go to the library and see if we can find him in a book about Kentucky reptiles."

We backed away and made a wide circle around

the tree. The lizard watched us warily, but he didn't come after us.

Hiking through the forest, we didn't see anything else out of the ordinary. We accidentally spooked a deer that had been hiding in the brush, and when he leapt up and bolted off, Jillian and I both nearly jumped out of our skins.

I kept my eyes peeled. I really wanted to find that old, abandoned graveyard, but I couldn't get that silly monster-lizard out of my mind. In fact, that's how I thought of the creature: *monster-lizard*. It was so unlike any other lizard I had ever seen. Certainly much bigger, except for the ones I'd seen on television and in zoos. When I was in first grade, we went on a field trip to a zoo and I saw a Gila monster, which is the only venomous lizard that lives in the United States. They grow to be about two feet long. They can't move very fast, so they're not really a danger to humans, unless someone is intentionally trying to catch them. However, they only live in the Southeastern part of the United States, and there aren't very many of them left.

But what we'd seen in the tree wasn't a Gila monster, and it drove me crazy trying to think of what it could be. Certainly not a chameleon or a salamander or a skink.

Weird. Just plain *weird*.

I looked at my watch. "We should be getting back," I said to Jillian. "Mom wants us home for lunch."

"We'll just have to keep looking," Jillian said. "That old graveyard isn't going to go anywhere."

"Yeah, maybe," I replied. "I might come out after lunch and look for it."

But there was something I wanted to do first, before we went on another hike in search of the old graveyard. I was going to find out what that monster-lizard was. Then, maybe I could find him again and catch him.

Then again, maybe the thing was dangerous. If he was lost from a zoo or a pet store, there was a good chance he was from another country. Maybe the creature was venomous, like the Gila monster. Maybe it was vicious, and bit people.

And that's exactly what I was thinking, hiking through the forest, on our way home . . . when I felt a sharp pain dig into my lower leg!

4

The bite on my leg surprised me so much that I stumbled forward and nearly fell. I turned and scrambled away, ready to face the charging lizard . . . and got the surprise of my life.

"*Gotcha!*" Katrina Holland said as she stood from her hiding place. She had been crouched down behind a tree, beneath a tree branch, waiting for us.

"You!" I exclaimed. "I'll get you back for that!"

"Fat chance," Katrina said with a smile as wide as the Ohio River.

"How did you know we were coming?" I asked.

I was a little mad, but I had to admit: she'd scared me pretty good. In that sense, it was kind of funny, thinking I'd been attacked by a monster-lizard. I certainly hadn't expected anyone to be hiding behind a tree in the woods.

"Your mom told me you went for a hike," Katrina said, getting to her feet. She had leaves tangled her black hair, and she pulled them out. "I didn't know if I'd find you or not, but I thought I'd give it a try. Did you find the old graveyard?"

Jillian and I shook our heads. "Not today," My sister said. "I'm beginning to think this whole thing is just a wild goose chase."

"It's out there somewhere," Katrina said. "My dad said he found it when he was little, but that was a long time ago, and doesn't remember where he found it."

"We *did* find something pretty strange," I said. "A lizard of some sort."

"So?" Katrina said with a shrug. "There are lizards all over the place."

I shook my head. "Not like this one. This one was a lot bigger than the ones we usually see." I explained to Katrina what it looked like. She listened intently, puzzled.

"I've never seen a lizard like *that* around here before," she said.

We followed the trail home. It was just before noon when we got back, and the three of us were sweating in the late morning sun. Katrina and Jillian made plans to meet after lunch. Katrina's family has a pool in their backyard, and they were going to hang out there for the rest of the day.

"You can come, too," Katrina said to me.

I shook my head. "No thanks. I'm going to see if I can find out more about that lizard we saw."

During lunch, I told Mom about what we'd seen. She said she'd never seen a lizard like that before.

"It was really bizarre looking," Jillian said. "He hissed at us."

"Very strange," Mom said.

Jillian finished her sandwich. "I'm going to put on my swimsuit and go to Katrina's" she said. "We're going to hang out by the pool."

"It's a good day for that," Mom said. "It's going to be hot this afternoon. Thank goodness we have air conditioning."

Jillian got up and went to her room, and I

continued telling Mom about the lizard.

"Why don't you use the computer in my office and see if you can find him on the Internet?" she said.

My eyes widened. "That's a great idea!" I replied.

I finished my sandwich, gulped down a glass of lemonade, and hurried into her office.

"Don't touch anything but the computer," Mom called out from the kitchen.

"I won't," I hollered back as I sat at her desk. Mom is a neat freak, and she can't stand it if one thing is out of place . . . especially in her office.

I heard Jillian's bedroom door open. "See ya later, Mom," she said.

"Have fun," Mom replied. Then I heard the front door open and close.

Seated in front of Mom's computer, I went to a search engine and typed in the words 'lizard,' and 'Kentucky.' Tons of sites came up. I browsed the images, but I didn't see any lizard that looked like the one we saw in the forest. The only ones that came up were smaller, maybe five or six inches long.

So, I tried another search, this time simply typing in the word 'lizard.' Twenty-one million, nine hundred results were returned! I'd be searching for hours, if not days!

I quickly scanned the first few pages of images, but I didn't see any lizard that looked like the one we'd spotted. I was about to give up, but I clicked on one more page.

And there it was.

I pulled my hands away from the computer keyboard, and stared. I was stunned . . . especially when I saw what kind of lizard it was.

"Mom!" I called out excitedly. *"Mom! Come here! You've got to see this!"*

"Give me just a minute," Mom called out from the kitchen. "What did you find?" I could hear cupboard doors opening and closing as she put dishes away.

"You're not going to believe it!" I replied. "It's not a lizard . . . it's a *dragon!*"

"A dragon?" Mom said as she appeared in the doorway.

I pointed at the computer monitor and turned to look up at her. "This is it, right here!" I said, tapping the screen.

Mom moved closer and leaned down. "A baby

Komodo dragon?" she said suspiciously. "Are you sure?"

"That's exactly what we saw," I replied. "That's what it is! A baby Komodo dragon!"

"But they don't live in Kentucky, do they?" Mom asked.

My eyes darted back and forth as I scanned the details on the monitor. "No," I replied. "They don't even live in the United States, except in zoos. That's what it says here, anyway."

"I wonder what a baby Komodo dragon is doing in Paducah, Kentucky," Mom wondered aloud.

I shook my head. I was puzzled, too. "You've got me," I replied. "Maybe he escaped from a zoo. Do you need your computer, right now?"

"Not just yet," Mom said, but I've got to get back to work soon."

Mom went back into the kitchen, and I continued to read about Komodo dragons. Turns out, they aren't really 'dragons,' but lizards, just as I'd suspected. Baby Komodo dragons climb trees, where they are safer. But as they grow, they get too big to climb trees. In fact, Komodo dragons can grow to ten feet in length, and weigh over three hundred pounds!

Komodo dragons are the largest living species of lizard in the world.

But here's the weird part: they only live in Indonesia, which is thousands and thousand of miles from Kentucky.

How did a Komodo dragon get Paducah, Kentucky? I wondered. The most obvious answers, of course, where the ones we'd already come up with. Either the reptile was someone's pet that got away, or it escaped from a zoo . . . which seemed the most likely answer, as the lizard is protected under government law, and people aren't allowed to keep them.

So, what zoo? I wondered. *We don't have a zoo in Paducah. There's one in Louisville, but that's a long ways away.*

And right then, I had another idea. Now that I'd found out what the creature really was, I began to hatch a plan to catch him.

My mind spun. *I'll be famous!* I thought. *I'll catch him, and then I'll call the newspaper and television stations!*

I was so excited that I got up from the computer and raced to my bedroom, thinking about what I would need to catch the baby Komodo dragon. I didn't read anything more about the lizard; I just wanted to catch him and show him off. Sure, I'd probably have to give him to a zoo, but that was okay. He'd be safe there. Maybe they would even name him after me!

Jason, the Komodo dragon.

Very cool.

But, as I was about to find out, I should have read more about Komodo dragons. I only read a little bit about them, and I didn't know what they ate, I didn't know where they slept. I didn't know how aggressive, fierce, and dangerous they could be.

But I was going to find out . . . the hard way.

ABOUT THE AUTHOR

Johnathan Rand is the author of more than 50 books, with well over 3 million copies in print. Series include **AMERICAN CHILLERS, MICHIGAN CHILLERS, FREDDIE FERNORTNER, FEARLESS FIRST GRADER,** and **THE ADVENTURE CLUB.** He's also co-authored a novel for teens (with Christopher Knight) entitled **PANDEMIA**. When not traveling, Rand lives in northern Michigan with his wife and three dogs. He is also the only author in the world to have a store that sells only his works: **CHILLERMANIA!** is located in Indian River, Michigan. Johnathan Rand is not always at the store, but he has been known to drop by frequently. Find out more at:

www.americanchillers.com

Dont Miss:

WRITTEN AND READ ALOUD BY JOHNATHAN RAND!
AVAILABLE ONLY ON COMPACT DISC!

Beware! This special audio CD contains six bone-chilling stories written and read aloud by the master of spooky suspense! American Chillers author Johnathan Rand shares six original tales of terror, including *The People of the Trees, The Mystery of Coyote Lake, Midnight Train, The Phone Call, The House at the End of Gallows Lane,* and the chilling poem, *Dark Night.* Turn out the lights, find a comfortable place, and get ready to enter the strange and bizarre world of **CREEPY CAMPFIRE CHILLERS!**

ONLY 9.99!
over sixty minutes
of audio!

Order online at
www.americanchillers.com
or call toll-free: 1-888-420-4244!

Don't miss these exciting, action-packed books by Johnathan Rand:

Michigan Chillers:

#1: Mayhem on Mackinac Island
#2: Terror Stalks Traverse City
#3: Poltergeists of Petoskey
#4: Aliens Attack Alpena
#5: Gargoyles of Gaylord
#6: Strange Spirits of St. Ignace
#7: Kreepy Klowns of Kalamazoo
#8: Dinosaurs Destroy Detroit
#9: Sinister Spiders of Saginaw
#10: Mackinaw City Mummies
#11: Great Lakes Ghost Ship
#12: AuSable Alligators
#13: Gruesome Ghouls of Grand Rapids
#14: Bionic Bats of Bay City

American Chillers:

#1: The Michigan Mega-Monsters
#2: Ogres of Ohio
#3: Florida Fog Phantoms
#4: New York Ninjas
#5: Terrible Tractors of Texas
#6: Invisible Iguanas of Illinois
#7: Wisconsin Werewolves
#8: Minnesota Mall Mannequins
#9: Iron Insects Invade Indiana
#10: Missouri Madhouse
#11: Poisonous Pythons Paralyze Pennsylvania
#12: Dangerous Dolls of Delaware
#13: Virtual Vampires of Vermont
#14: Creepy Condors of California
#15: Nebraska Nightcrawlers
#16: Alien Androids Assault Arizona
#17: South Carolina Sea Creatures
#18: Washington Wax Museum
#19: North Dakota Night Dragons
#20: Mutant Mammoths of Montana
#21: Terrifying Toys of Tennessee
#22: Nuclear Jellyfish of New Jersey
#23: Wicked Velociraptors of West Virginia
#24: Haunting in New Hampshire
#25: Mississippi Megalodon
#26: Oklahoma Outbreak

Freddie Fernortner, Fearless First Grader:

#1: The Fantastic Flying Bicycle
#2: The Super-Scary Night Thingy
#3: A Haunting We Will Go
#4: Freddie's Dog Walking Service
#5: The Big Box Fort
#6: Mr. Chewy's Big Adventure
#7: The Magical Wading Pool
#8: Chipper's Crazy Carnival

Adventure Club series:

#1: Ghost in the Graveyard
#2: Ghost in the Grand
#3: The Haunted Schoolhouse

For Teens:

PANDEMIA: A novel of the bird flu and the end of the world
(written with Christopher Knight)

Johnathan Rand travels internationally
for school visits and book signings! For
booking information, call:

1 (231) 238-0338!

JOIN THE FREE AMERICAN CHILLERS FAN CLUB!

It's easy to join . . . and best of all, it's FREE!
Find out more today by visiting:

WWW.AMERICANCHILLERS.COM

And don't forget to browse the on-line superstore, where you can order books, hats, shirts, and lots more cool stuff!

All AudioCraft books are proudly printed, bound, and manufactured in the United States of America, utilizing American resources, labor, and materials.

USA